NICK AND JUNE WERE HERE

ALSO BY SHALANDA STANLEY

Drowning Is Inevitable

SHALANDA STANLEY

NICK AND JUNE WERE HERE

ALFRED A. KNOPF *New York*

Visit us on the Web! GetUnderlined.com

Educators and librarians, for a variety of teaching tools, visit us at
RHTeachersLibrarians.com

Library of Congress Cataloging-in-Publication Data
Names: Stanley, Shalanda, author.
Title: Nick and June were here / Shalanda Stanley.
Description: First edition. | New York : Alfred A. Knopf, 2019. | Summary: Told in two voices, Nick, a sometimes artist who steals cars to support his aunt, and June, who has been hiding her symptoms of schizophrenia, run away together.
Identifiers: LCCN 2018026942 (print) | LCCN 2018034010 (ebook) |
ISBN 978-0-399-55660-9 (ebook) | ISBN 978-0-399-55658-6 (hardback)
Subjects: | CYAC: Runaways—Fiction. | Schizophrenia—Fiction. | Mental illness—Fiction. | Automobile theft—Fiction. | Artists—Fiction. | Love—Fiction.
Classification: LCC PZ7.1.S735 (ebook) | LCC PZ7.1.S735 Nic 2019 (print) |
DDC [Fic]—dc23

Printed in the United States of America
February 2019
10 9 8 7 6 5 4 3 2 1

First Edition

For my mother, who read to me since birth
and always changed the endings
when she knew I needed her to

CHAPTER 1

JUNE

It was midnight and we lay on our backs in the bed of Bethany's truck. We were in the middle of a cornfield and it was after harvesttime, so it was just the three of us and the leftover broken stalks. There was supposed to be a meteor shower that night. We'd been watching them together since we were in elementary school, back when we'd watch from my trampoline with my parents sitting on the swing on the porch, back when we thought the meteors were shooting stars and we'd make wishes.

Nick checked the time on his phone. "It should start any minute now," he said.

That was his job, to check the time. Nick made sure things happened when they were supposed to.

The night was clear and the sky was so huge it felt infinite, so big that I felt the weight of it.

The world feels too big. Sometimes the world feels so big you can't breathe.

My breath hitched and my fingers jerked, reaching for the edge of my notebook that lay next to me. I never let it get too far away. I'd gotten better at not reacting when it happened, but I had to write it down before I forgot the words. I sat up.

The world feels too big. Sometimes the world feels so big you can't breathe, I wrote.

"Hey, lay back down," Nick said.

Not yet. "What time is it?" I asked him.

"12:03," he said.

12:03, I wrote.

Nick and Bethany didn't ask what I was writing. They were used to my documenting. They were used to everything about me. Bethany and I had been together since birth, born only a day apart. She came first. Nick had been in my class every year since kindergarten, but we didn't start spending time with each other until the fifth grade, when we were assigned to work as partners on a social studies project. Our project was called "Cotton: Then and Now." It was a long and arduous task. Secrets were spilled. Bonds were forged.

Bethany nudged me. "Is it happening again?" she asked.

I nodded. It happened more and more.

She pulled me down to them. "Keep your eyes on the stars," she said. "They are so beautiful."

They are so beautiful.

She felt me flinch and turned to me. "It's okay," she said.

They are so beautiful they are SO beautiful.

"I'm with you," she told me. Her breath on my cheek was warm and smelled like coconut. Bethany always smelled like sunscreen and reminded me of summer.

And she was right. The stars were beautiful. I imagined what Earth would look like if I was on a star and looking down at it.

The world feels too big.

I imagined sitting on the star and looking down at Earth. I'd hold up my thumb and close one eye so the whole world disappeared behind it.

I squeezed the notebook to my chest. Sometimes I could just hold it and feel better. Nick scooted closer to me so that his leg touched mine. He knew when I needed him to touch me.

A year ago, things had changed between us. One day, every time I looked up, he was looking back at me, and then I caught him drawing my face in the margins of his history notebook. He drew all the time, but he'd never drawn me before. When I asked him about it, he said, "I just feel better when I'm looking at you."

His dad had gone to prison two years earlier and Nick had been sad ever since, so I was glad something was making him feel better. We started spending more and more time together, just the two of us. He'd come over and we'd sit on my porch swing. My parents didn't know what to think of it, so I'd bring a textbook outside with me. We could all pretend it was just homework. Nick would even ask me a question or two. At first we sat on opposite ends of the swing, but every day he'd sit a little closer, until we sat so close that our legs touched. Once he pulled a sucker from his pocket. It was root-beer-flavored, our favorite, but there was only one. We shared it, back and forth from his mouth to mine. That was how things changed between us. It was a few gained inches on a front-porch swing and that sucker. He told me things he'd never told anyone, the kinds of things you'd confess only in the dark. It was a powerful feeling, and I was addicted.

He noticed things about me that others didn't. Some were big and some were small. He noticed that the time we almost had a wreck, I covered my ears instead of closing my eyes. It was the same way with scary movies, in the everybody-is-about-to-die parts. I'd much rather see it than hear it. He knew I didn't read books with animals in them, just in case they didn't survive the story, and I didn't eat yellow food, not because I thought it was gross but because yellow was my favorite color and I thought the world needed more of it, not less. After our first fight, he snuck into my house while my parents and I were out for dinner and painted one of my bedroom walls sunlight yellow. My parents didn't appreciate his apology like I did.

He was the first person to realize something was wrong. He knew before I did.

I noticed things about him, too. His pinkie finger on

his right hand was crooked for reasons he couldn't remember and he prayed before he ate, but only a soft mumble so nobody would notice. It was the same thing when he did something nice for someone. It was small gestures, so if you weren't watching closely, you'd miss it. That was Nick. He never wanted to reveal his true self. When his mom left town with her boyfriend and he had to go live with his aunt Linda, he started saying, "I'm okay," before anyone had a chance to ask him how he was doing.

The first night we kissed, we were on my back porch. He reached out to touch my hand, and even though he'd touched my hand more than one million times before, this touch felt new. Everything about that night felt new—new porch, new sky—and when his eyes met mine, a brand-new Nick and June. Our lips touched and I swear to God there was an electric shock, a tiny blue light that jumped from his body to mine. He'd felt it, too, because he stumbled back. It was like the universe was sending us a message, a *zap* blessing. Bethany said it probably wasn't anything so dramatic, just static electricity built up between our bodies.

"Do you want one?" he asked me now, holding out a red Sour Patch Kid. He always saved the red ones for me.

There was a whole section in my notebook titled "How Do You Know When Someone Loves You?" I wrote it because I was pretty sure he loved me, and not in the I've-known-you-all-my-life-of-course-I-love-you way but in the you-make-it-easier-to-breathe-when-you're-around-me way. He'd showed me with his actions in a thousand different ways and I'd written down all of them. It was my proof that *love* was a verb.

We worried Bethany would be weirded out by our relationship or feel left out, but she wasn't. "I've seen this coming," she said. It wasn't unusual for her to see things before we did.

It did change things, though. Now it was usually me and Bethany, or me and Nick. Tonight was special, to have both of them in the same place at the same time. That happened less and less, and not just because Nick and I were boyfriend and girlfriend but because Nick spent a lot of time doing other things. He'd made choices neither Bethany or I agreed with. He was following in his dad's footsteps, like maybe if he did bad things he'd understand his dad better, or maybe if he did bad things but was still mostly good, then his dad was still mostly good, too.

I was pretty sure his choices were leading him down a dangerous path, and I didn't know what that meant for the three of us.

"Pass the blanket," Bethany said.

It was chilly. Nick pulled a blanket across us and we waited for the show to start.

"Would you rather eat only cold foods or hot ones?" Bethany asked.

She didn't like it when it was quiet for too long.

"Cold," Nick and I said at the same time.

"Would you rather have the one thing you've always

wanted and die tomorrow, or never get it and live forever?" she asked.

"Do I know I'm never going to get it?" I asked.

"Does it matter?" she asked.

"Yeah," I said. "If I don't know, then I'd rather live forever, trying to get it. If I know, that changes things."

"I see your point," she said.

"Would you rather go to school naked or get a bad grade?" Nick asked.

That one was for Bethany. She'd made all A's our whole lives.

"It would suck to go to school naked, but I'd totally do it."

"Would you rather be able to see into your own future or somebody else's?" I asked.

"Mine," Bethany said.

"I don't want to know what's coming for anybody," Nick said.

"Really?" I asked. "Not even a ten-minute glimpse, like a little heads-up?"

"Remember that time the two of you came to a middle school dance dressed like flapper girls, because Misty Wright convinced y'all that when the invitation said 'Dress Up,' it meant costumes, not nice clothes?"

Whenever would-you-rather conversations took a turn Nick didn't like, he deflected with embarrassing memories of our childhood.

Bethany leaned up so she could see him. "And you wore a

dress because you couldn't resist taking the invitation liter-
ally."

We laughed and it was the only sound for a mile.

Nick and Bethany helped me keep the secret. They were
as scared as I was, so they helped me hide it, covering for me,
making excuses. "She's just tired," they'd say. "She's fine,"
they'd promise. We knew that once everyone knew something was wrong, it would change everything. We knew that
they wouldn't let us keep things the way they'd always been.

*You could never stop this. You're only going to get worse,
worse, worse.*

I sat up.

You could never stop this. You're only going to get worse, I
wrote.

"What time is it?" I asked Nick.

"12:07," he said.

12:07, I wrote.

I wrote down what happened most every time it happened, at least the times when I was sure it was happening.
Sometimes it was hard to tell. I kept everything in my notebook. I'd always been a record keeper, so I was creating a
timeline of the details, hoping I could make sense of what was
happening.

Nick sat up. "It's okay," he said.

This was their favorite thing to tell me.

"It's not okay," I said. "You don't know what this is like."

"Umm, I can imagine."

But he said it like a question, and *umm* was what he said right before he lied.

He rubbed my arm up and down, whispering close to my ear, "You don't have to be afraid if I'm with you." This wasn't a question or a lie. He didn't understand how I could be scared of anything if I was with him. He looked at me like he could see all the way inside. "It's us against them, remember?"

I studied his face, the tiny scar that ran through his right eyebrow. Sometimes when he said just the right thing, I focused on his flaws so I wouldn't get tricked into thinking he was perfect.

"There," Bethany said, pointing.

We turned our heads and saw the first meteor streak across the sky and then another one and another one. The sky put on a show of light and flame, and I heard the music.

"You're missing it," Nick said. "Stop writing and watch."

The corners of his mouth turned down, but I pretended not to notice. I pretended I couldn't hear the worry in his voice, because I had to write the song down, the one they couldn't hear. This was the part I liked.

There was a wistful quality to it, like the song was telling me to remember this moment. A part of me thought that this was just my imagination, that there was no music. The other part knew the truth. It was my own private orchestra, chords playing in time with the light show and building to a climax. I knew the peak was coming even though it was a song I'd never heard before. I felt the crescendo building from inside me.

Don't forget what tonight feels like.

The music crashed to a stop and my heart crashed with it. The good parts never lasted long.

Don't forget what tonight feels like, I wrote.

Nick scooted closer. He put his hand on top of mine so I had to stop writing. "Look," he said.

A meteor flew across the sky like someone had shot it out of a cannon, the tail of it sparking.

"Make a wish," Bethany said.

Star light, star bright, the first star I see tonight.

I pulled my hand out from under Nick's and turned away from him.

Star light, star bright, the first star I see tonight, I wrote.

"What time is it?" I asked him.

"12:13," he said, his voice quieter.

12:13, I wrote.

I wish I may, I wish I might.

I closed my eyes and wished for quiet, clamping my hands over my ears even though I knew it wouldn't help. The sound was coming from inside me.

Have this wish I wish tonight.

"You're shaking," Bethany said. She put her arms around me like she could keep me still.

I couldn't stop this anymore, never could.

This has been coming for a long time.

The voices weren't my first symptom.

Creed, Arkansas, had 5,570 people in it and forty-five churches. For a town that small, that was a lot of Jesus. There were five churches on the walk between my house and school, one with a sign that said SPIRIT-FILLED, making me wonder what was inside the other ones.

School wasn't a straight shot from my house. There were two lefts and two rights. A left on Raymond Street, a right on Powell, left on Walton, right on Green. Left, right, left, right, like an army march. I'd walked this path most every day, every school year since first grade. It'd been a couple of weeks now since I'd done it, though. Nick and Bethany had asked me not to walk to school anymore, not after what had happened when I'd ended up at Becky Wilkes's house. Nothing good had ever happened at Becky's house. I'd promised them that I'd ride with one of them, but Bethany was late and Nick wasn't answering his phone. I didn't drive. Three thousand two hundred eighty-seven people die in car crashes every day. There were too many variables to consider when driving and I didn't trust myself to handle them.

The sidewalk was busted up with too many cracks to count. I passed houses with cars on cinder blocks in the front yards and dilapidated signs advertising things I couldn't make out, the letters rusted. Once, my cousin Tanya came to visit from Atlanta and pointed out all the wrecked parts of Creed, like I couldn't see them. I didn't tell her that it was a cover, that we kept the good stuff hidden so outsiders would keep driving by. If you came to Creed, we wouldn't tell you about the color of the winter wheat fields when they were at full height, or what it felt like to stand on Purple Rock in July and turn your face to the sun. You would never know about the abandoned barn hidden in the woods where anything could happen. We kept those things secret, because Creed had a finite number of resources, and the people born here got first dibs.

We had five legitimate employment options. You could work at a lumber mill, a school, a farm, the hospital, or, of course, a church. My parents worked at the hospital. My dad was one of the administrators, but he had been a family doctor before that, and my mom was a nurse. If you wanted to do anything else, you had to get out.

I was dying to get out. Bethany was, too. She'd memorized bus schedules, because no way was her truck going to make it as far away as we wanted to go.

Graduation was a couple of months away and the deadline for choosing which college Bethany and I would attend was looming. We'd applied to fifteen colleges and we'd heard back from almost all of them with yeses. We were smart. That left me only a few months to convince Nick to leave town when we did, only a few months to figure out what was wrong with me and fix it. I didn't know where we would go. I'd stayed up nights thinking about it. It had to be someplace where new things happened. Nothing new had happened in Creed my whole life, but I really couldn't blame Creed for that. This town wasn't a place for beginnings.

I had no idea what I wanted to do with my life—unlike Bethany, who'd been saying she was going to be a nurse anesthetist since elementary school—but my mom promised that college was a good place to figure it out.

When I was in the second grade, Mrs. Shirley had made us write a "When I Grow Up" essay and she said I had to pick something to be. I didn't have to stick to it but I had to write something down. I chose teacher, but probably just because I was under pressure and she was in the room with me. In the fifth grade, I was convinced that I'd make an excellent lawyer. "You'll argue with the wall," my mom would say. And then there was the marine biologist phase, and that time I thought I was going to be a dancer even though I'd never taken lessons. When you're eight and say you want to be an astronaut, people give you indulgent smiles and think it's cute, but when you're seventeen, they expect you to be more practical.

I made lists in my notebook of possible occupations. Lately I'd added photographer and writer to the list. I didn't know if I'd make a good writer, but I was good at making lists in my notebook.

The only thing I knew for sure was that I loved school. I loved everything about it—the order, the expectations, the time frames. It came with a definite beginning and end. So I knew college was in my future, even if I didn't know what I wanted to major in. My mom said that it was okay to try everything before settling on something for good. She made college sound like a closet with all these different Junes and I could try them all on until I found one that fit.

I heard Bethany's truck before I saw it. The muffler broke noise violation codes even though Nick fixed it about once a week. The truck was older than our combined ages. She loved it.

She plowed down the road, stopping next to me. She rolled her window down, frowning. Bethany was an excellent frowner.

"You were supposed to wait for me," she said. She was mad.

"You said you wouldn't be late."

"You don't always have to be on time. It's character-building to be late for things sometimes."

"Then you should have a really strong character."

The corner of her mouth lifted. "Will you please get in my truck?"

She'd been coaxing me into her truck since we were fifteen.

I got in, slamming the heavy door after me.

"Is there a reason you're here?" she asked, gesturing with her head toward the window.

I looked around. We were on Walton Street, by the pharmacy, nowhere near the school.

"You're lucky this town only has seven streets," she said, "or I wouldn't have been able to find you."

It was two lefts and two rights. Left, right, left, right. It was the sidewalk. The cracks had led me here.

"Don't tell Nick," I said.

She gave me side-eye as she slid the truck into drive, but if one of us was going to cave and tell my parents that something was wrong, it was him. I'd seen the warning in his eyes when he'd found me at Becky's.

"I'll add this to the list of things we don't tell Nick," she said.

It was a short list, but there were things he didn't need to know.

My mom and Bethany's mom were best friends and had timed their pregnancies so they'd be pregnant together. The day that Bethany was born before me was the only one we'd spent apart. Our parents raised us like we were one person and rarely referred to us by our names, calling us "the girls" instead.

"Are the girls going to the lake?"

"Where are the girls?"

"Tell the girls to come inside."

Thank God they finally let us dress in different clothes. It was at least second grade before the kids in our class realized we weren't actually twins. This was funny because we were total opposites. Where I was shy, she was bold. I was an observer. Bethany was a doer. I liked the dark. Bethany was the light. She shone on everything and everyone around her. You couldn't hide anything from her, because a light sees everything.

She handed me a brochure. "Look at the back," she said.

It was a brochure from Southeastern Arkansas University.

I flipped it over and there was a bulleted list of all the ways it was awesome and the clear choice for our future.

"Their water-ski team has been national champions for twenty-eight consecutive years," she said.

"You don't water-ski."

"So? That's impressive. Not many schools can claim that."

Some people picked colleges based on their academic reputations, or the cost of attending, but Bethany examined them by their prowess at water sports.

"But this is in Mackenzie," I said.

"So?"

"I thought you wanted to go somewhere farther from home."

Mackenzie was only a three-hour drive from Creed.

"It's not a terrible idea to stay closer to home."

I wondered what had changed her mind. Maybe it was me. Maybe she knew I was unraveling and it was better to be close to home when I came undone.

"Did you know that tug-of-war used to be an Olympic event?" Bethany asked.

She knew when I was too deep in my head.

"You're making that up," I said.

"Why would I make that up?"

"Because you're you and that sounds like something made up."

"Well, it isn't, and I think they should bring it back. I mean, they kept curling."

We pulled up to school and she parked in her usual spot. The place next to it was empty.

"Don't worry," she said. "You know he doesn't show up until at least third period."

Nick barely came to school anymore but that didn't mean I wouldn't worry. Twice before when he hadn't come, it was because he'd been arrested. Bethany and I had spent only one day apart but Nick and I had been separated for much longer periods of time.

Creed High School was the only high school in town. There were eighty-seven kids in the senior class and our faces were framed and smiling in the hall next to the office. Every year, Mr. Lewis, the principal, hung the seniors' pictures. He called it his hall of fame. I wondered what happened to the photos after graduation and imagined a special locked room stacked with years of senior portraits. I hoped they were organized by year.

AP English, world history, AP government, lunch, AP physics, AP calculus, office. I spent the last hour of the school day answering the office phone so Mrs. Livingston, the school secretary, could take a late lunch. That was my day and every day looked pretty much the same. AP English, world history, AP government, lunch, AP physics, AP calculus, office.

Third period came and went and still no Nick, but then I remembered the art room. Sometimes Nick parked behind the school and went straight there. When he did come to school, that was where he spent most of his time.

The room was dark except for the light coming in through the windows. Nick was the only one in the room, his back to me. Mr. Nelson, the art teacher, was in his office in the back. Nick didn't notice I'd come in. He didn't notice much else when he painted. He'd been working on the same piece for a while now. It was a painting of the ocean. Nick had never been to the ocean. Most of his paintings were of places he'd never been, like he was imagining a life he didn't have yet.

He was absorbed in what he was doing, his brow furrowed. This wasn't the ocean with the waves crashing onto some shore with white sand beaches, but the ocean where the middle met the horizon and there was nothing but calm water and sky.

My shadow fell across the painting and he paused. I stood between the window and him and he turned to me. Sometimes he looked like no one took care of him. You couldn't tell this from his clothes or hair—it was a look in his eyes. He held out his hand to me. His hands were my favorite part of him. They were almost always dotted with dried paint, tiny flecks of color on his skin. I put my hand in his and our fingers laced together. Our hands knew just how to fit. We'd been holding them a long time.

He was so tall that I had to drop my head back to look at him. He'd shot up in the last couple of years. I'd gone to every high school dance with him since we were freshmen. In the beginning, the three of us had gone together. Each time, Mrs. Susan, who wasn't an actual photographer but had a good camera, took pictures, and my mom bought one every year.

"For posterity," she told me. If you lined up the photos next to each other, you'd see Nick grow taller in each one. I looked pretty much the same in all of them. There hadn't been much growth for me since I was fourteen, and I was trying not to be bitter about it. All of my changes were happening on the inside.

"Shouldn't you be in class?" he said. His voice was rough, like this was the first time he'd used it today.

"Shouldn't you be?"

He shrugged and turned back to the painting. He always looked at his paintings like they were problems he had to solve. Sometimes he looked at me like that, too.

"I think it's finished," I said.

"They're never finished."

The fourth-period bell rang, except it wasn't a bell. It was chimes this time. Mr. Lewis tried out different sounds to announce the ends of classes. The chimes were much better than the time he thought it would be a good idea to play music. They were all songs from the classic rock radio station. He'd stand in the hall as we switched classes. "These were the songs of my youth," he'd say, and rub his big belly. Every time he reminisced about his youth, he touched his stomach.

"June?" Nick asked. His voice sounded worried. His voice sounded worried more and more lately. "Did you hear me?"

"No," I said.

"We need to go," he said. "Mr. Nelson has a class this period."

Ping.

There was a sound, like something small and metal had been dropped at my feet. I looked down but didn't see anything.

Ping, ping.

"Hey," Nick said. His touch on my arm was warm. "Are you okay?"

"Yeah, let's g—"

Ping, ping, ping, ping, ping, ping, ping, ping, ping, ping, ping.

It felt like they were spilling from me and I clamped my mouth shut. I looked down again but there was still nothing there. My hands started sweating.

"June?"

The temperature in the room rose twenty degrees. I was burning.

"Are you okay?" he asked again. "Your face is really red."

"I'm fine," I said, pulling at my collar. This was my best lie.

I dropped to the floor and ran my hand along the surface, needing to feel something that would explain it.

The door to the art room opened and the lights flashed on, the sound of feet walking into the room almost drowning out the pinging.

"What are you doing?" Nick asked, squatting down next to me.

"I think I dropped something," I said.

"I don't see anything," he said.

"I need to find it." The pinging rang in my ears.

Nick mimicked my movements, running his hand across

the floor, even though I was pretty sure he thought it was all in my head. He was on his knees now.

I was in the hall before I remembered making the decision to make a break for it. Nick stood next to me. It was cooler here. The pinging didn't follow me into the hall and my heartbeat slowed. One beat, two beats, three.

The other kids in the hall moved around us like we were the rock in the river, Nick's face stuck in a worried expression, his hand in mine, squeezing.

"Let's get out of here," he said. Nick's default setting was escape. Anytime anything got sticky, he was ready to run. He motioned with his head toward the side exit. He always saw the quickest getaway. Even when he parked his car at my house, he faced it out, toward the street, just in case.

"I don't think that's a good idea," I said.

"Probably not," he said, "but let's go anyway. I'll have you back before school's out." Pulling me toward the door, he said, "We'll go to the barn." The smile spread on his face, his attempt to lure me. "There's this thing I want to do to you."

Because we were going opposite the direction of the other students, we attracted the attention of Mrs. Bingham, the librarian, who was always in the halls instead of the library. She cocked her head to the side like she was asking a question. I stopped.

With one hand on the door, Nick looked back at me and mouthed, "Let's go."

I squeezed his fingers in mine, two quick squeezes for *yes*.

It was a system we'd worked out a long time ago, two for *yes*, one for *no*.

He threw the door open and it banged against the outside wall. No point in sneaking when someone watched you. I gave Mrs. Bingham a polite wave and Nick pulled me into the light.

He drove a car he'd built by himself. His dad had been a mechanic and taught Nick everything he knew. There were some things I wish he hadn't taught him.

I had never spent much time with his dad. There was this one time his dad had taken us to the circus. The school had handed out free tickets earlier that week and Mr. Hawthorne volunteered to give us a ride. I had never really liked the idea of the circus because I always felt sorry for the animals, but in Creed, when someone gives you a free ticket to something, you go. He let me sit in the front seat. I'd never done that before. My parents followed all of the suggested safety rules when it came to airbags, seat belt standards, and height.

I couldn't remember one thing about the circus that day, but I could tell you about the smell of leather on the seat of his car and the feel of the door handle in my hand, because I'd held on like it was an amusement park ride. Mr. Hawthorne had flipped down the visor on my side because I kept holding up my other hand to shield my eyes from the sun. I was at least a foot too short for the visor to work, so he took his sunglasses off and put them on my face. That was what I remembered, pulling into the parking lot of the Civics Center, one hand gripping the door handle, the other on the too-big sunglasses so they didn't fall off my face.

Nick pulled to a stop in front of a field just outside town.

"We're here," he said. He announced it every time we came to the barn.

When we stepped into the thicket, I heard the birds. It sounded like hundreds of them but I couldn't see them. I looked to Nick to see if he heard it, too, but his face didn't give anything away. We moved farther into the field and they rose into the sky in one *whoosh* movement, stopping both of us. They were blackbirds and they moved in unison, swooping left, then right, and finally up, up, like they all shared the same mind. Their wings beat and blocked out the sky, their song rising in pitch as they went higher and higher.

"Do you see this?" I asked.

He squeezed my fingers twice and pulled me along, toward the barn's doors, in a hurry to get inside. The barn was a place where the outside rules didn't apply. It was a place where we could just be. There weren't too many places for us like that.

It was my favorite place in the universe, a space built more than fifty years ago with wood from a species of tree that no longer existed in Creed. They had cut down what was left of the shortleaf pine to build this place. When I'd first found out, I'd been sad, but the more time I spent in the barn, the more I appreciated the trees' sacrifice.

The barn was dilapidated, with a metal roof. It looked

abandoned but the truth hid inside, just like it did in Creed. We'd been coming here since the beginning of sophomore year. The summer before that, when Nick went to visit his uncle in the Ozarks, his uncle had told him about it. His uncle was from Creed, too, but had left town right after high school. He said it was a place we could use when we needed to get away. It was a way to get away for people who couldn't go anywhere.

When Nick opened the doors, the colors were the first thing I noticed—blues, greens, reds, and so much yellow. The walls were covered in murals that Nick had painted. Bethany and I had helped with some of them. We didn't know what we were doing, but we could follow directions.

He led me to the ladder that went up to the loft. "Be careful," he said.

Most of the murals in the loft were of the Ozarks, because that was Nick's favorite place. He'd painted every view of the mountains from his uncle's cabin, where he'd spent most of his summers. I tried not to let it bother me that Nick's favorite place was somewhere I'd never been.

The loft looked more like a deserted bedroom than anything else. There was a cot in the corner and a record player, a rug, and on one wall, a shelf stacked with Nick's art supplies. Nick had bought the record player to replace the one his uncle had left behind, which stopped working a long time ago. It ran on batteries, and every time I played a record, it felt like going back in time.

When his uncle was a teenager, he'd come here all the time. He hadn't left just his record player behind, but all of his records, some of his clothes. It looked like he'd left suddenly and hadn't known that he'd never be back. His name was Hank and he was an artist, too. He was the one who'd taught Nick.

Some of the artwork in the barn was Hank's. He hadn't painted on the walls, though. He'd hung canvases around the loft. There were so many of them. He took off right after his eighteenth birthday and he'd never been back. He left them all behind and moved to the Ozarks. I knew he lived alone and had never married.

"Why doesn't he come back home, even for a visit?" I'd asked Nick. "Why did he leave everything?"

Nick would just shrug, though, and never answer.

Hank's things were spread all over the loft, mixed in with mine and Nick's. That was another reason I loved the barn so much. I liked the idea that our story lay on top of his, even if I didn't know what his story was, even if sometimes it felt like we were trespassing.

Nick went to the records and pulled one from its sleeve and set it to play. All of the music was old, like the songs of Mr. Lewis's youth, so I rarely recognized anything. The songs had one thing in common, though. They told stories, and sometimes I got so caught up in them that I didn't hear what Nick was saying.

He stepped closer to me, his eyes never leaving mine. The

floor creaked as he moved. The loft floor was old. One day we were going to fall through.

His eyes held a question and I knew what it was. He was leading up to the real reason we were here.

"Can I paint you?" he asked.

He didn't mean a portrait. Nick saw art in everything and painted everywhere, on every space, but I was his favorite canvas. His fingertips were the brushes. His palm was the palette.

"Yes," I said. The answer to that question was always *yes*.

Even though he'd done this at least a dozen times before, I always felt nervous, like it was the first time. I sat down on the cot with my heart in my throat and tried to remember what color my underwear was. It didn't stand a chance at matching my bra, because I didn't own a matching set, but maybe I hadn't put on the Teenage Mutant Ninja Turtles pair. It was now or never and I lifted my dress over my head.

Beige. It was beige. Boring was better than weird. He studied the lines of my body, and my heartbeat sped up. His eyes hit my curves, my stomach, appreciating. No matter how many times I took off my clothes for him, he never took it for granted, like he worried that it might not happen again.

"You're perfect," he said.

He said it like he believed it and it made me feel brave. I lay down on the cot.

He stood over me. "What should I paint?" he asked.

"The blackbirds," I said.

There'd been so many of them, their wings flapping, their bodies moving independently but going the same direction. My thoughts were like the blackbirds and I hoped they could all go the same way, too. I wanted them on me.

He squatted down to me, then reached out and touched a scar on the inside of my ankle. It had happened at marine biology camp when I wasn't paying attention to the guide who warned me not to step into the water because of the shells. "They cut like glass," he'd said.

All of my scars had origin stories. Unlike Nick's—he couldn't remember how he'd gotten most of his.

"I'll start here," he said.

He followed the line of my scar around my leg, then lifted my leg with one hand as he trailed his finger around my calf with the other, marking the birds' flight path. Goose bumps popped out on my skin, the song in the background singing about hungered touches. His fingers wound around my leg and up my side. When he reached my middle, he lightly pressed both hands against my stomach side by side, his thumbs touching, marking the wingspan of one bird. I held my breath. He continued the birds' path up my chest, his fingers touching spots that no one but he had claimed. He lifted my hair and traced around my shoulder. He raised his eyes to mine for approval. I nodded.

Squeezing the paint he wanted into his hand, he noticed my leg jumping. "You'll have to be still," he said.

He said it like it was an easy request, but sometimes being

still was the hardest thing of all. Sometimes it felt like I was being chased by all the things I couldn't explain. Being still meant there was a better chance they could catch me. The hair on my arms stood as I thought about it. I'd left my notebook in the car and my fingers trembled.

"Are you cold?" he asked.

I shook my head.

"You sure?"

"Do you think I'm crazy?" I asked.

Sometimes it was best to get it all out there. I was already in my underwear. This was just another layer exposed.

The light in the loft filtered in through a window near the roof, highlighting the dust particles floating across the room and past his face. Waiting for his answer felt like being cut open. Right down the middle.

"You're not crazy," he said.

"What's happening to me?" I asked.

"I don't know," he said. "We'll figure it out, though." Nick was always pragmatic. "Maybe it's time to tell your parents. Your dad's a doctor. He'll be able to help."

"It'll change everything," I said. "Once they know. They're parents. They're not going to let something like this slide. They'll make it a huge deal."

"Maybe it is," he said.

"But I don't want it to be. I want what I've always wanted and I don't want anything to change." The idea of them finding out made me feel frantic. There was no way that my parents could know and my life still continue in any recognizable way. I wanted to keep things the same for as long as I could.

"Hey," he said, his voice soft. "Let's just think about this moment right now. And right now I want to paint blackbirds on you, so be still."

He dipped his finger in black paint and dragged it up my leg, the coolness soothing me. Nick's paint was the salve and I tried staying still so he could paint the pieces of me back together again.

It almost worked, but then I was back to fidgeting.

"Remember that time we rode the train to El Dorado?" he asked.

I rolled my eyes at him, because how could I forget that.

It hadn't been a passenger train. The cars were empty and Nick showed me all the different graffiti. He talked about the colors and brands of spray paint that worked best and how you could tell all these things by the curves in the tags. My parents thought I was spending the night with Bethany, so we had the whole night. It was the first one we'd spent together. Nick knew the train's schedule and that it went to El Dorado to pick up more cars and then would ride back through Creed on its way to wherever trains went when they rode through Arkansas.

"Remember how scared you were when the train started moving?" he asked. "You've never held my hand so tight, and you started talking about how bats are descended from dragons."

"I ramble when I'm scared."

"I know."

He reached out, placing his hand on my still-twitching legs. "Talk to me now."

I knew this was his attempt at distracting me so he could paint, and I wanted it to work but I didn't want to talk about bats.

"There was a girl and a boy and they lived on top of a mountain," I said, looking at the roof, at one of the paintings of the Ozarks. "They did all the things you tell me you do in the summers with your uncle."

"Like what?"

Nick had told me stories of hiking and fishing all day and never catching anything, but he'd made it all sound wonderful.

"They carried fishing poles to a perfect spot. He tried teaching her how to hook a worm and didn't make fun of her when she refused to do it."

"What was his name?" Nick asked.

"Robert," I said.

"And hers?"

"Mary."

I watched as he painted wings around my calf. His hands were strong and hard but they could create something as delicate as a blackbird's wings.

"Mary thought he was beautiful," I said.

He smirked, like he thought a boy being beautiful was

funny. His jeans scraped against the barn floor as he scooted closer to me, and my mouth went dry.

"What did Robert think about Mary?" he asked.

"He thought she was beautiful, too. And smart. They lived on the mountain and Robert hunted and Mary—"

"Cooked and cleaned?"

"No," I said, and slapped at his shoulder.

He smiled full on now and I relaxed into the cot. His tactic was working.

"Keep talking," he said.

"Do you like it so far?"

"Yeah, but I kinda miss the dragons."

"There was a dragon. Mary rode it every morning, checking the perimeter, making sure no one could get through their fences."

"Why were they trying to keep people out?"

"Because the world worked better when it was just the two of them."

"You mean the three of them."

"Yes, the three of them. Robert, Mary, and the dragon."

His fingers paused and he cleared his throat, his foot tapping like he was nervous. *Tap, tap, tap.* His eyes were the color of the ocean he had painted in Mr. Nelson's art room.

"This summer, when I go to my uncle Hank's," he said. "I want you to come with me."

I'd never been invited before.

"We could do everything you just said, except there's no

dragon. You'd love it." His eyes were hopeful, like he was selling me on the idea. "And John will be home this summer. He'll be there, too." *Tap, tap* went his foot. "If you want to see him before you and Bethany leave for college."

John was Nick's brother. He was a few years older than us and had been in Afghanistan for the past year.

"I'd love to come," I said.

Nick seemed relieved that I'd agreed to go, his fingers going back to painting, his breath exhaling slowly, like he'd been worried I'd turn him down.

I didn't know how I felt about John being home this summer. Nick and John were really close. When they were younger, Nick didn't go anywhere without him. And when he left, I watched Nick fold in on himself, one piece at a time. I was still trying to unfold him in places. We hadn't talked about John much since he'd been gone. When I'd bring him up, Nick always changed the subject. Talking about John made Nick worry about him more.

John had been gone a couple of years now, for basic training and then Afghanistan. He hadn't hung out with us all that much, except for his last summer in Creed, right after basic training and right before he was deployed. There was a flood and there were parts of town that were completely underwater. Some people lost everything. Nick and John came back from Hank's when they found out about it. John was good in a crisis, always assessing the situation and coming up with a plan. He led the charge on town donations. I remembered where I was standing when I found out he was being sent away. We were in front of the school, because that was where people were dropping off their donations of food and clothes. Mr. Moore, the school janitor, clapped John on the back and said, "We're proud of you, son. You'll be fine over there." My stomach hit my feet when I realized what he was talking about. Suddenly John seemed taller. Nothing made you feel like a kid more than when you stood next to someone who was about to fly across the world to spread freedom, or whatever it was we were spreading in Afghanistan.

We spent his last weeks in Creed doing everything he wouldn't be able to do once he was gone. We stayed up late watching movies, eating ice cream, hanging out in the barn. We picnicked after swimming in Lake Brady so he could get baked by the sun on Purple Rock one more time. When he didn't think anyone was looking, he took a rock and carved *John was here* on it. I caught him writing it everywhere, on the wall at the movie theater, on one of the tables in the diner, on the walls of the barn. I tried not to let it make me sad that he was reminding everyone that he was here.

It seemed like a good time to do things we'd never done before but had always wanted to, like jumping off the high rock into the lake. John volunteered to go first. He wasn't scared to be the first one to try something.

"I need to get to your back," Nick said now, pulling me from the cot.

He led me to the center of the loft where the light was

better. Pulling a ponytail holder off my wrist, I put my hair up so it wouldn't be in his way. He turned me where he wanted me and I came face to face with one of Hank's paintings of the mountainside.

I was excited to go to Hank's. I'd been imagining what it might be like for years. Maybe Bethany could go with us. It would be weird to take a trip without her. I'd never done it before and she'd want to see John, too. I knew Hank didn't like having a lot of people around, though, and a secluded cabin in the woods probably wasn't the best place for Bethany, who couldn't stand the quiet.

"What happens next in the story?" Nick asked.

It took me a second to remember what he was talking about.

"Robert spent his days trying to impress Mary, so she'd fall more and more in love with him," I said.

He moved behind me, outlining the birds flying up my body. I couldn't see him, only feel him, his fingers, his breath.

He turned me to face him.

"What can I say right now to make you fall for me?" he asked.

"I've already fallen for you."

He dropped to his knees and I held my breath as his hands moved against my rib cage. The look of concentration on his face was the one he got only when he painted, and I fell harder.

When he was done, he took my fingers and turned me

slowly, checking his work. Of all the things he'd painted on me, this was my favorite. I wanted to keep it on me forever, but it would be an extreme first tattoo. Nick grabbed a paper towel and tried to get the paint off, but I kept turning, the sunlight that streamed in through the loft window hitting my body, the light playing with my eyes. I couldn't stop looking at my skin. I was a swirling mix of blackbirds and girl. If I spun, it looked like the birds in the field, flying higher, higher.

"Come here," he said.

"Why?"

I didn't want to stop spinning.

He reached out, grabbing my hand and pulling me to him. His hand was in my hair, holding me close but trying not to smudge the paint. Painting on me always led to kissing. His lips touched mine. Kissing him felt like sitting at the top of a roller coaster. His tongue slipped into my mouth and we went over the edge. It felt like the birds were flying up my body. I held on to him so I didn't fly away, too.

I pressed closer. Nick's mouth was the only soft part of him. His T-shirt was white and the blackbirds' feathers marked it where I pressed against him. His phone buzzed with a text message but he ignored it, bringing me closer, the blackbirds flying from my body to his. It buzzed again and again. Nick stepped away from me and checked it. The birds stilled. There was only one person who would keep texting like that.

"Benny?" I asked.

He nodded. Nick couldn't ignore Benny. Benny Robertson owned a garage downtown, but it was a front to a chop shop and Nick was his best guy.

"We gotta go," he said, sad.

"No, we don't. We can stay right here. You don't have to do what he says."

"But I do. He's my boss."

"He doesn't have to be."

"Stop," he said.

"Why do you do it?" I asked.

His face shut down like it did when a teacher asked him a question in class. "You know why."

"No, I know why you used to, but not anymore. You've more than paid him back by now."

When Nick's dad went to prison, he'd left owing Benny a lot of money. Nick and John had been expected to work at the garage until they'd paid off their dad's debt.

"John left. You can, too. And when Bethany and I go away to school, you can come with us," I said. I liked pretending that I wasn't falling apart and that my plans wouldn't be interrupted by whatever was happening to me.

"I'm not going to college."

"I know that, but you can still come with us."

"Where will I live?" he asked. "I can't stay in the dorms."

Whenever I tried talking Nick into something he wasn't sure about, he tried to discourage me with logic.

"You'll get an apartment, a small studio."

"How am I paying for this apartment?"

"You said you had some money saved."

"Not that much," he said.

"Enough for a security deposit and the first month's rent," I said hopefully. "You'll have enough to get started and you can get a job as a real mechanic."

He turned away from me and started putting his paints away. "You say it like it's easy."

"It *is* easy. You put in an application. You go to the interview. You get the job. You're good. Anyone will see that." But maybe that wasn't why he was reluctant. "I'll help you with the application if that's what you're worr—"

"Stop pretending I'm like you," he said, slinging his brush at the shelf in the corner. It glanced off and clattered to the floor. "You're the one with choices," he said.

Picking up my dress, he tossed it to me. I pulled it over my head. Goodbye, birds.

"You don't have to steal cars for some asshole that doesn't care about you," I said.

His look said not to say anything else. Nick had started working at the garage as an obligation, but I didn't think that was what it was anymore. There was a part of him that liked what he did.

CHAPTER 2

I was six years old the first time my dad got arrested. Me and my brother, John, were in the car with him. We didn't know it was stolen. He'd picked us up from school in it, saying he was taking it to Uncle Benny's garage so he could fix it. We took a lot of cars to Uncle Benny's. It was where my dad was his best self. In the garage, there were problems he could solve. People looked up to him there, asked him questions that he had the answers to.

He taught us everything he knew about cars, how to build them, how to break them down, how to fix them, and, later, how to steal them. "You gotta make a living," he'd say. Benny was always in the background, lurking. It'd be a few years before we realized he wasn't our uncle.

I remembered everything about that day. I wore an

orange-and-white-striped shirt and it had ketchup stains on it because I wasn't good at opening those little packets they gave you in the cafeteria. John sat next to me in the back seat. He was three years older than me and was already doing his homework, because he knew there wouldn't be time once we got to the garage. We hadn't been in the car long when I heard the siren. Dad sped up, taking a turn too fast, and I spilled over, landing in John's lap. John righted me and looked out the back window, already sweating. He'd looked worried ever since Dad had pulled up to the school, though, like he knew it was going to be a bad day.

"It's right behind us," John said.

I could tell from John's voice that he was scared, my first clue that I should be, too. We took a few more turns and I gripped the seat, but not hard enough, because I fell onto the floorboard. When I got back in my seat, I met my dad's eyes in the rearview mirror. John was on his knees now, facing out the back window.

"There's two of them now," he said.

Dad slowed down the car, like he had thought he might be able to outrun one police car, but never two.

We pulled to the side of the road and he slid the car into park, his eyes still on mine in the mirror.

"I'm sorry," he said.

Worry added to my fear, because he'd never apologized before.

Dad turned to face us in the back seat. The lights from the

police cars bounced off the insides of the car, making his face flash blue and red.

"Don't move and don't say anything to them," he said. He looked only at John now. My parents did that a lot, looked at John when they needed to make sure we both understood something important.

The cops must've run the plates, because they already knew the car was stolen. They walked up to the car with their guns drawn. When the cop on my side of the car saw me and my brother in the back seat, his face changed, his gun lowered. We were a surprise.

"Step out of the car," he said to my dad. "Keep your hands where I can see them."

The other cop was a woman and she didn't take her eyes off me and John.

The first cop opened my dad's door. My dad moved slow, just like the cop said, kept his hands up, like he was told. The cop pulled him away from the car as soon as my dad stood up, saying things I couldn't hear. Then he was pressed down, face against the hood. I sat up on my knees so I could still see him.

"Sit down," John said. "He said not to move."

But I didn't listen, because I needed to see him. Both cops were talking to him now and he was saying something back, his lips moving fast. His eyes met mine again and his mouth stopped moving, time stopped moving. He took a deep breath and shook his head. The cop yanked him up and turned him away from us, leading him to one of the police cars. I turned in the seat, tracking his every move until they put him in the back of the car and I couldn't see him anymore.

The panic set in, because I felt like as long as I could still see him, everything would be okay. As soon as he was out of sight, my nose burned and I tried not to cry, because I wasn't a baby.

"What are they gonna do with us?" I asked John. "What are we gonna do?"

John looked like he thought it was up to him, in that moment, to figure out the rest of our lives.

The woman police officer opened the back door on my side. She had a look that a lot of grown-ups had when they saw me and my brother. I'd be a lot older before I realized what that look meant. She felt sorry for us.

"It's going to be okay," she said. "Let's go for a ride."

We didn't move. We'd been taught to be afraid of them.

"Don't believe that shit they tell you at school," my dad would say. "Cops are not your friends."

She squatted down so she was eye level with us, her hand reaching for us, but she knew better than to touch us.

"Everything is going to be all right," she promised. "We'll take a ride to the police station and we'll call your mom. She'll come pick y'all up. Nobody is going to hurt you."

I waited for John to decide if we should trust her. John looked wary but then he nodded and moved toward her, scooting me along the seat with him.

She smiled and took my free hand. John held the other one.

"It'll be a quick ride," she promised. "I'll even let you play with the siren. Would you like that?"

I nodded and John squeezed my hand. He didn't say anything, but the look on his face warned me not to be a traitor.

It was my first time riding in a police car. It wouldn't be the last.

June sat as far away from me in the car as she could get. I tightened my grip on the steering wheel, fighting the urge to try and fix it by saying I was sorry. Apologizing wouldn't help when it came to this fight and June was tired of hearing those words anyway. She wanted actions.

It wasn't June's fault that she thought I could be different. She'd always been told she could be anybody and do anything, so it was no surprise that she believed it. The problem was she believed it so hard that she thought it applied to other people, too.

One of the blackbirds peeked out of the neck of her dress, and I wanted to touch it but I knew she wouldn't let me. Seeing her wear my paint did things to me. The times she let me paint on her were the top moments of my life. It was my two favorite things—painting and touching June—combined into one activity.

I'd always been able to draw. It came naturally. Painting didn't. My mom's brother, Hank, had taught me how. Mom had been sending us to spend summers with him since me and John were little. It was the best thing she ever did for us. Hank was everything my dad wasn't. He lived in a cabin in the Ozarks that he'd built himself. He had a workshop behind the cabin where he built furniture and painted. Summers with Hank were some of the best parts of my life. I couldn't wait for June to meet him. I would've invited her before now, but Hank was wary of who came to his cabin. It'd taken me a while to convince him that June was someone he could trust.

She kept her face turned toward the passenger-side window, not looking at me. When she was mad at me, it was the worst thing she could do. I'd rather her yell or throw things, hit me, anything but not look at me.

The first time I spent any time with her outside school, we were in the fifth grade. We were in the parking lot of the bowling alley. June's parents had dropped her off at a birthday party. It must have finished early or June's parents were late picking her up, because she was outside waiting for them. I was with my brother and his friends. We spent a lot of time in that parking lot. My brother's friend Michael Lawson had started this bicycle gang called the Tarantulas. We were all too young to drive, hence the bicycles. They let me in because they'd wanted John, and John didn't go anywhere I couldn't go. The Tarantulas ran things from the bowling alley on Olympic all the way to North Seventh Street. Other kids knew better than to bike anywhere near there. We'd ride back and forth, stopping at Ken's Quickstop to steal grape sodas, before meeting in the parking lot of the bowling alley. We'd hang out all day, flipping off cars as they drove by.

June was sitting on the bench right outside the door, looking everywhere but at the kids on the bikes, because she'd been warned about us. Everyone had. A couple of the guys started giving her trouble, riding in circles right in front of her, calling her names. The easy thing to do was ignore it, but I couldn't. And anyway, I owed her. We were in the same class at school and the teacher had made us work together on a project. That was when she found out that I was shit at reading, another thing I got from my dad. I'd worried that she'd laugh or tell people, but she just read everything for me and let me design the display board.

Jason Patrick kept riding closer and closer to her. He was big for his age and was the worst one of us. When he circled even closer to her, I threw a rock at his spokes, making him crash his bike. He wasn't hurt and it didn't damage his bike, just made him fall off of it. Everyone laughed and he jumped up mad and came right at me. I thought about riding away but I worried he'd take his anger out on June, so I jumped off my bike. His fist came quick and smashed into my nose. It wasn't my first fight. I got at least two punches in before we were pulled apart. June's dad stood between us, keeping me and Jason separated. As soon as her dad dropped his hands, Jason and the other Tarantulas took off, leaving me and John and my bloody nose in the parking lot.

June told her dad what had happened. He squatted down so he could get a better look at my nose and told John to go inside the bowling alley and ask for some ice. John came back outside with a Ziploc bag of ice and June's dad pressed it against my face.

"I don't think it's broken," he said. "But you need to get it cleaned up. Keep pressure here," he said, and pinched my nose. "So it'll stop bleeding." He looked like he was proud of me. I didn't get that look a lot, at least not for doing something good.

"Fighting is never a good idea," he said. "But thanks for sticking up for my girl." He stood and looked at John. "I don't have a place to put your bikes, but I can give you a ride home, help clean him up."

"That's okay," John said. "We'll be fine. I can clean him up."

June's dad nodded and they got in their car and drove away, June smiling at me through the window of the back seat like she was glad to know me.

After that day, I found excuses to be wherever she was. I wanted that feeling again, that feeling of being good. She was an enigma, because she shouldn't have wanted to be my friend but she did.

Her hand was on the seat between us now and I put mine next to it, testing the waters. I could close my eyes and draw her hands from memory. Her fingernails were painted purple and chipped. The artist in me couldn't ignore it. A song came on the radio and I knew it was one she liked because she moved her head in time to the music. It was a movement almost too small to notice. I turned the radio up. We came to a stop sign and I took a chance and covered her hand with mine. She looked at me, finally.

There was so much wrong in my life, but none of that mattered when I got to be near June. She had a way of making everything seem like it was going to be okay, even me. She made it safe for me to tell the truth. I'd confessed so many things to her already.

My phone buzzed with another text message. I'd meant to silence it. I'd ignore it, but Benny wouldn't stop. Reluctantly, I let go of her hand and dug my phone out of my pocket.

Get your ass to the garage. Now.

June grabbed it from me.

"Do you know how many people get into accidents because they were reading texts?" she asked.

No, but she did. June had a thing for numbers and facts. Even more so now. She'd stopped trusting herself, so verifiable facts were important. She texted something back and tossed my phone into the back seat.

"June," I sighed.

I'd pay for that text later. Her look dared me to say something about it. One step forward. Two steps back.

"Are you hanging out with Bethany later?" I asked.

She nodded.

Bethany was June's best friend, but they were more like

sisters. They could read each other's minds. I'd witnessed them have whole conversations with looks only.

"Will you be at your house or hers? I could come by after," I said.

She shrugged and then flinched. She leaned down and grabbed her notebook and a pen from her bag and started writing.

Something was going on with June and I didn't have a name for it. It had started a couple of months ago. She was the most solid of the three of us, the one we turned to when things went sideways, but lately it was June that was sideways.

She'd stopped sleeping. The bags under her eyes were a constant now. She heard things sometimes, things that no one else heard. There was one time I was pretty sure she saw something, too. She was at Becky Wilkes's old house. She'd walked there instead of school. Bethany had called me, worried, because June was late and wasn't answering her phone. Unlike me, June never missed school. She was up for the perfect attendance award at the end of this year, and I mean perfect attendance in that she'd never missed a day of school since first grade. She loved it.

It'd been Bethany's idea to look for her at Becky's—she said June had been talking a lot about her lately. Mr. Wilkes wasn't home, and it was a good thing, because that guy was a real asshole. We heard June's voice when we got out of my car. It came from the backyard. She was talking and it was animated, like she was upset. When we came around the side of the house, June stopped mid-sentence. She looked surprised to see us and then mad. Probably because we'd interrupted her.

"What are you doing?" Bethany asked.

At first June crossed her arms like she didn't want to answer and then finally said, "I needed to talk to Becky. It's private."

June was alone and no one had seen Becky in over a year.

The world got flipped in the moments when nobody said anything. It was the first time I worried that whatever was going on with June was something we couldn't control.

"Becky's not here," Bethany said. Her voice was small.

Becky Wilkes was a girl our age. We'd gone to school together our whole lives but I'd never talked to her. June had, though. They were friends. Becky had run away during spring break the year before.

June glanced around the porch and then looked flustered. Then she gathered herself and said, "Well, I know she's not *really* here. There's just some stuff I wanted to tell her and I thought this would be a good place to do it."

"Except it's not," I said. "Her dad could've been home and you don't want to be anywhere near him."

There were a lot of rumors about the things that had happened at Becky Wilkes's house and none of them were good. It'd just been her and her dad. I never knew where her mom was or what had happened to her. Everyone seemed kind of relieved when Becky left, thought she was better off. They sure as hell didn't look very hard for her.

"We should go," Bethany said. "We need to get to school before the end of first period."

June nodded but she looked reluctant. She didn't want to leave but she followed us. She kept looking back at the porch, though.

Bethany and I rationalized her behavior. Anybody'd see things if they'd gone that long without sleep.

I snuck her some of my aunt Linda's sleeping pills that night. "Don't take more than one," I said.

"Are you sure that's enough?"

"Believe me, it is."

I was almost excited when I gave them to her—we both were, because we thought if she could just sleep, she'd wake up like the old June.

We thought it'd worked. For a while, she seemed okay. But then I couldn't get her any more pills without my aunt noticing, and night after night, she slept less and less. Whatever was happening snuck back up on her.

She flipped a page in her notebook. "What time is it?" she asked.

"2:54," I said.

She wrote it down.

Pulling into the school parking lot, I parked next to Bethany's truck. School would be getting out any minute now. June stuffed the notebook into her bag.

"I'll call you later," I said.

She didn't say anything, just got out of the car.

Shit.

"Hey," I said, leaning over the seat so I could still see her face.

She paused and looked back at me, her hand resting on top of the door, her chipped purple nails tapping, like she didn't have time for this. The sun was at her back, casting a shadow across the car's seat and highlighting the blue around her eyes. They were bruised with no sleep. Even this tired, she was beautiful.

"Tell me something new," I said. "Something nobody else knows."

I'd been asking her that every other day since forever. I collected facts about her because I wanted to know more about her than anyone else did.

At first I thought she wasn't going to say anything, but then she said, "You have choices, too."

She shut the car door and walked away from me, my blackbirds flying up her legs.

My phone buzzed from the back seat—another text from Benny, probably. I didn't bother getting it, just left the school parking lot and thought about my choices. It buzzed again and I pressed down on the gas pedal and got my ass to the garage like Benny wanted. Benny wasn't someone I needed to piss off. Everyone knew that, my dad especially.

Dad had been convicted of grand theft auto for the third

time, and now it'd be twenty-two years, three months, and two days before he'd see sunlight from outside a fence. When he went away, that was when me and John had gone to work for Benny. Dad was in deep with Benny and it was up to us to pay him back. We didn't know what would happen if we refused and we thought it was best not to find out.

Everyone in town knew who Benny was and what he did and that if you wanted your oil changed, you took it somewhere else. They also knew that all of Benny's guys ended up in jail eventually. That wasn't how I wanted to leave town, but for most guys like me, that was the only way we got out. It was just where we went after high school. I'd already been to juvie twice.

Deep down, June knew that. John had, too. That was why he'd joined the army on his eighteenth birthday. He had been deployed a year later.

"Stay out of trouble," he'd said.

He quit Benny's for me before he left, but he hadn't counted on our mom meeting Larry and leaving town for good. Mom was a waitress at the Blue Hill Diner and Larry was a truck driver who came through town from time to time and always sat in her section. He was a big tipper and Creed didn't have many of those, so he made an impression.

John didn't know that I'd have to move in with Aunt Linda, our dad's sister, or that Aunt Linda would need help making rent. And if I was telling the truth, I wasn't good at staying out of trouble. I didn't know the right way to get the things I needed. It just made sense to keep working for Benny. I knew guys made real money working for him, but I wasn't as careful as I should've been. John hadn't been in basic training a month when I was arrested for the first time.

I'd lived with Aunt Linda for a couple of years now. Mom took off right after John left for basic training. I tried not to be mad at her for leaving. Some days I managed it. Logically, I understood. She saw her chance to get out of here and she took it. Aunt Linda didn't see it the same way. "What kind of mama leaves her boy?" she'd ask me. But I'd known it was coming. Since I was ten, she'd been taking off, a summer here, a winter there. She was like a runner training for a marathon. Like she was adding one more mile at a time, she left and stayed gone for longer and longer, until she'd built up the stamina to leave for good.

She wasn't a bad person. More than once she'd bought art supplies with food money, but nobody had ever put her first. When she finally met someone who did, she didn't want to let him go.

Now my unofficial job title was the Car Thief of East Third Avenue. Lately I'd thought about quitting like June wanted. We were free from my dad's debt and I had some money saved. I almost had quit once or twice but then Aunt Linda would come to me and say, "They're cutting the lights off today if I can't pay the bill," and I'd do what had to be done. On my side of town, guys didn't wait to grow up to take care of their families. That was something I couldn't make June understand. Even though we grew up in the same town, we didn't live in the same world. There was a dividing line in Creed and I lived on the wrong side of it.

Quitting always seemed like some lofty dream anyway. I couldn't remember life before Benny's Garage. Me and John were practically raised there. There were marks on the inside of one of the storage room doors, tracking our heights over the years.

Our lives were divided between the garage and Hank's cabin. We were very different people in each place. At first it was hard for John to adjust to being at Hank's in the summer, because Hank treated us like kids. He didn't expect John to make decisions. John had to decide everything when we were in Creed. Mom was always working, and before Dad was sent to prison, he was in and out of county jail, so John was left in charge. It was a pretty sweet setup. We didn't have a bedtime. Nobody made us brush our teeth. We even drank Coke with breakfast.

Tommy Henderson was standing outside the garage with a smile too big for his face. I could always judge how bad it was at the garage by the size of Tommy's smile. The bigger the smile, the worse things were. It was a coping strategy. Tommy was the only Tarantula that I still hung out with. He was a year older than me and lived in my neighborhood. His dad had run off two years ago. Tommy came to work for Benny right after that. Benny collected all the fatherless kids in town.

Tommy motioned for me to stay in the car. Opening the passenger-side door, he said, "Finally. Benny's pissed. He's been trying to get you for over an hour. He wants us to go to Macomb tonight." He plopped down in the seat. "I'll ride with you. It'll save us some time."

We drove to Macomb, a town forty-five minutes away. The deal was two cars a month and the only rule was that we didn't steal in Creed. "We don't shit where we eat," Benny said.

I drove around until dark, scouting, with Tommy talking nonstop about some girl named Lanette that he loved. Tommy loved a lot of girls.

"What happened to Avery?" I asked.

"Aww, man. Her mom met some dude from Benton and they took off."

Her mom was smart.

We found what we were looking for just after the sun went down. There was an older-model Cavalier parked next to Lake Murray. It looked like it'd been there awhile, because it had flyers advertising different things stuck under the windshield wipers. I made a couple of loops around the lake and then parked down the street. Older cars were easier for a lot of reasons. The locks were easier to pop. They were simpler to hot-wire, and had no alarm systems. In Creed, Benny never had trouble moving older parts.

Reaching under the seat for my tools, I said, "Don't start timing me until I get to the car."

Tommy grinned. We were competitive. My best time was four minutes and thirty-eight seconds, seven seconds faster than his best time. John held the record among all of Benny's boys, four minutes, and if anybody was going to break it, it was going to be me.

Tommy scooted into the driver's seat when I got out. He'd follow me back to the garage.

I looked around for anybody watching, but this time of night on this side of town, the only people around were trying to score or the homeless. Neither cared if I stole this car. I walked up to it, trying not to think about what June had said about me not having to do this. It wasn't good to be distracted.

The lock pick was light in my hands. I slid it between the window and door, lifted, and I was in. I dropped into the seat like the car was mine and leaned down, popping the steering wheel column open. I found the wires I'd need, my dad's words running through my head. *You can't just go grabbing at shit. All the wires are live.* I stripped the wires like I'd done a hundred times. I rubbed them together and the car came to life. I looked around to see if anyone had paid attention to the cranked car but no one had.

You're gonna be better than me. It was John's voice this time. Sometimes I imagined that John was with me when I did jobs. He'd appear in the seat next to me, like he was already a ghost, reminding me what I needed to do next.

Checking the mirrors, I pulled out onto the street and

clocked Tommy pulling out behind me. I used to keep track of how many cars I'd stolen, but lately I'd lost count. I'd been stealing cars before I had a license to drive them.

The road always felt different after doing a job for Benny. I felt every bump in my stomach, noticed every broken streetlight, each passing car. When you drove a stolen car, you had to remember everything you knew about driving. All of the rules mattered, but some were more important than others. Make sure you didn't follow the car in front of you too closely. Come to a complete stop at stop signs, none of those rolling ones. Put your blinker on a hundred feet before making a turn. Working brake lights were very important. That was what got my dad the last time. It was a broken taillight that got him pulled over, his third strike.

I checked the rearview mirror to make sure it was Tommy behind me and no one else. I missed his blabbering. It was too quiet and too easy to think about all the things I tried to avoid thinking about—the future being my biggest worry. June and Bethany were taking off as soon as they could and I didn't know what to do about it. I didn't want June to go, but she wasn't asking my permission and she was never mine to keep. I'd always known that. It still hurt. That was the main reason I wanted to bring her with me to the Ozarks this summer, to spend more time with her before she left Creed and never came back.

Part of me wanted to go with her when she left, but there was only one other place I could see a life for myself and that was in the Ozarks with Hank. This summer I was planning on asking him if I could stay for good. I'd been thinking about it for a while. That might be my only real chance at breaking free from Benny. I'd be 250 miles from Creed and Benny's Garage. I could start something new there. Maybe if June could see that a person could have a life there, she'd be able to see a life for herself there, too.

Crossing into the town limits, I passed Plywood Sawmill. It was one of four mills in town. It was where Uncle Hank had worked before he left. In Creed, trees were big business. The sawmills were where guys like me who didn't end up in jail went to work. If you couldn't get ahead with your education, you did it with your back. Sawmills were dangerous, though. No one had been killed in a long time, but more than a few men walked around town with limps.

When I pulled back into the garage, Benny was standing just outside his office, his arms crossed. His face was in a scowl, but that was his usual look.

He looked over the car as I got out. "You did good, kid," he said.

I tried not to let it feel good but I couldn't help it.

Tommy came inside the garage and tossed me my keys and then lifted the car's hood. A couple of guys came over and they started stripping it.

Benny pointed at the paint on my shirt. "You were with that girl today when you couldn't answer your phone?" he asked. He liked asking questions he already knew the answers to. "That explains the last text I got from you. Don't let her distract you from what you need to be doing. She'll be out of here soon and you'll still need a job. So unless you want to work at one of the mills, don't let your dick make your decisions for you."

I clenched my fists at my sides, wanting to punch his words back into his mouth. I closed my eyes and imagined myself punching his words back into his mouth.

"I know what's important," I said instead. "I won't forget."

I wished I didn't need Benny, but I did. Tommy needed him. A lot of people did. Benny filled a gap that no one else in town did. People liked to look down on him and all of us who worked for him, because everybody knew what was up, but Benny stepped in when we didn't have other options.

He walked around the car, inspecting the guys' work. "Even though you went with him, this doesn't count as your car," he said to Tommy. Tommy didn't say anything back, just nodded, looking younger than he had earlier. Benny had that effect on him.

I usually stayed and helped break the car down, but that night I just wanted to get the hell out of there. As soon as Benny went back into his office, I said, "Hey, Tommy, I'm gonna slip out. I'll make it up to you later." Tommy grunted something from under the hood that I took as a yes.

My aunt Linda's house was a couple of blocks from the garage. It was a three-bedroom brick house that looked exactly like all the other houses on the street, except for the shutters. Everybody's shutters were different colors. It was the one thing you got to pick when you moved in.

Aunt Linda's car was in the driveway when I pulled in. I was surprised by this. She worked the late shift at the hospital on the cleaning crew.

The screen door creaked when I opened it, and she turned to face me. She was in front of the stove, working on something. She usually left supper for me so all I had to do was warm it up.

"I didn't expect to see you before I left for work," she said. She had a huge grin on her face, like this was a good surprise.

"I ducked out of Benny's a little early."

"Well, ain't I the lucky one," she said, her smile showing her one dimple.

My aunt Linda used to be beautiful. I'd seen pictures of her and my dad when they were kids, before their worry lines weighed down their faces, before they had so much to worry about.

I dropped a kiss on her head. She smelled like bacon and fried eggs. Aunt Linda cooked breakfast no matter the time of day.

"You look tired," she said.

"I am."

"Grab us a couple of plates," she said.

We rarely got to eat a meal together. I usually didn't get home until after she'd left for work and I was gone in the mornings before she got home.

She brought everything to the table. "School will be out soon," she said, piling bacon on my plate. She phrased it like a question.

I nodded. She didn't mention graduation because we both knew that wasn't happening. I didn't have enough credits. I would've quit already, but school was a place to see June and I could use Mr. Nelson's art room.

"You going to Hank's again this summer?" she asked. She asked this every spring.

"Yes."

"What are your plans after that?" she asked.

I almost choked on my eggs. It was our first direct conversation about the future. She'd been tiptoeing around this topic for a while, though, always adding, "What are your plans after that?" anytime she wanted to know what I was doing that day.

"It can only go one way if you keep working for Benny," she said.

The way it went for my dad. Aunt Linda wasn't stupid. She knew who Benny was and what I did. She never questioned me, though. She couldn't afford to.

"I'm figuring it out," I said.

"Well, don't figure me into your plans."

"What do you mean?" I asked.

"I appreciate you helping out around here, but don't keep working there for my benefit. I'll figure something else out. I was thinking about getting a roommate. My friend Susan is planning on leaving her husband soon and she'll need a place to stay."

I'd been dreaming about moving to the Ozarks for a while now but didn't know how to put what I wanted into words. Or maybe I was scared to say it out loud, because then it'd be real. Maybe she'd sensed this. Maybe I didn't hide what I was thinking as good as I thought I did. Either way, I didn't know if I should be relieved that I wouldn't have to worry about her or sad because her financial stability depended on her friend Susan's divorce.

"You can go off on your adventure," she said, scooping eggs into her mouth. Then she leaned in close, until I could smell her perfume over the food, a weird mix of lilac and grease. "It won't hurt my feelings if you don't come back."

She leaned back in her chair and the kitchen light caught her eyes. That was the only reason I saw the tears in them. She was up and turned from me before I could react.

"Aunt Linda, nothing has to be decided tonight," I said.

She grabbed the washcloth from the sink and started wiping down the counter, not looking at me.

"You've got to get out of here," she said, her voice a whisper, like she was talking to herself instead of me. "Places like this aren't good for people like you. If you don't leave soon, Creed will grab on to you and never let you go, or worse."

Like my dad.

"You need to follow Hank's example," she said, pointing

at one of his paintings hanging on the kitchen wall. "He's been really good for you boys, showed you a different way."

The painting in the kitchen was of the view of his cabin from the hill behind the workshop, where you could stand and see the cabin and the forest behind it. From that angle, the Ozarks looked like an infinity pool, but instead of water it was trees. He would stand on that spot and say, "A man can really get lost up here." He'd say it like it was a good thing.

Most of Uncle Hank's paintings were landscapes. I'd only ever seen one that wasn't. I'd spotted it my first time there. It hung on the back wall of his workshop.

It was a painting of him and my mom when they were younger, standing in front of a house they never lived in, a two-story brick house with a picket fence.

"Paint is easy to manipulate," he explained. "You can make anything you want happen."

During that first summer with Hank, me and John helped him fix the fences that surrounded his property. As much as a couple of kids could help, anyway. Over time, we built rockers, picnic tables, nightstands, you name it. Sometimes I wasn't sure what we were working on, just put my hands where he told me and followed the steps he laid out for us. At night, I'd be so exhausted I'd fall asleep as soon as I lay down—and sometimes before, Uncle Hank waking me up at the dinner table and telling me to go to bed. He always made sure we had plenty to do.

I looked forward to going back every summer because I craved the feeling of everything having a purpose. If you wanted to eat, you had to hunt. If you needed a place to sit, eat, sleep, you had to build it. "There's no time for idle hands in the mountains," Uncle Hank would say.

Last summer was the only one I'd spent with Hank that John wasn't there for. That was probably why we'd fought so much. Me and Uncle Hank were a lot alike, which wasn't always a good thing. I thought about the last thing I had said to him and my gut twisted. I had a lot to apologize for before he would even consider letting me move up there.

Aunt Linda scraped the food she hadn't eaten into the trash can. "John will be home this summer."

It wasn't a question but she said it like one.

"Yeah, he's supposed to be," I said, handing her my plate.

I hadn't heard from him in a while, though, and I tried not to let it worry me. It'd been over two months since I'd gotten an email from him.

"That's good," she said. "I've been so worried about him, what with everything you hear on the news." She finished cleaning up and then turned to me and said, "I'm off to clean toilets. Let me know if you decide to stick around Creed after this summer. I can probably get you on at the hospital."

She knew I'd hate that. It was one more push out her door.

"Will do," I said.

"It doesn't pay as good as Benny, but there's no risk of jail time." She turned to me before walking out the door. "And it's a lot safer than working at one of the mills, but I know a union guy, too, so you just let me know. Okay?"

She didn't wait for me to agree with her, just pulled her purse strap over her shoulder and pushed through the screen door. Aunt Linda wasn't always subtle.

My phone rang. It was Benny. Just in case I needed another reason to leave town. He was probably calling to yell at me for leaving the garage early.

"Hey," I said.

"There's a car coming in the area in a few days," he said, surprising me. "It's special. I want you to get it for me. I'll pay double."

Sometimes I stole cars for their parts and sometimes I stole them for what was hidden inside them. I never asked what was hiding. The less I knew, the better.

Benny almost sounded needy, and he loved his money, so it was rare that he offered to pay more than usual. This car was important.

I wondered if I could really be different. It was one thing to daydream about a different life and another thing to take the steps to make it happen. Maybe I could do it. No time like the present. If so, I could use double.

"I'll do it," I said.

"Good. I'll get you the details when I get word that it's in the area."

"Hey, Benny," I said.

It was now or never. Aunt Linda was right.

"Yeah?"

It felt like there was a rock in my throat and I had to talk around it. "This is the last one."

He didn't say anything for a second.

"You joining the army, too?"

"No, I just don't want to do it anymore."

There was only silence and I watched the clock on the stove as the next minute ticked by.

"I'll see you tomorrow," he finally said. He hung up.

I could tell he didn't believe me. It didn't matter. I could be different.

I called June to let her know the good news, but she didn't answer. Neither did Bethany. I thought about driving to June's house, to tell her in person that I'd taken the first step, but I was beat. It took a lot out of a person to change.

The walls in my bedroom were covered from floor to ceiling. Aunt Linda had no rules when it came to decorating. I'd painted them every color, and then I'd started adding other things—paper, photos. The whole room was like a collage experiment that got out of control. Anytime somebody came over, they'd add something. Sometimes it was things they found in my room, other times it was something they brought with them. Once, June tore a page from her notebook and added it to the wall by my bed. It was blank. It was my favorite piece, though, because I knew how she felt about her notebook.

I liked to put the pictures of me and John next to the ones

of June and Bethany, like the four of us had a history, even though John had never really hung out with us all that much.

John was the one who had encouraged me to tell June I wanted to be more than friends. *Encouraged* probably wasn't the right word. He'd threatened to tell her if I didn't. I'm sure the fact that I'd kept bothering him over how to do it had something to do with his threat.

"You should just kiss her," he said. "You walk up to her. Look her right in the eyes so she knows what you're meaning to do and you kiss her."

"That's it? We shouldn't talk first? Tell her what I'm thinking?"

"What are you gonna say? 'Hey, June, I know we've been friends forever, but I can't stop thinking about you all the time, and probably not how you think about me, unless you've been thinking we should start hanging out without clothes.'"

"It wouldn't go like that," I said.

"Sure it would," he said, patting me on the back, his smile showing the gap between his front teeth.

When he joined the army, it had felt like a gut punch. He was the one person I had thought I could count on not to leave.

At first he emailed all the time. But then the emails came less and less often. Each one he sent felt like he was sending it from farther and farther away from home. I wasn't good at writing, so I sent him drawings instead, hidden in the care packages that Aunt Linda put together. The drawings were mostly of our favorite spot in the mountains. We'd found it together. Uncle Hank had taken us camping, and we'd hiked to a spot a three-day walk from his cabin. After a couple days, Uncle Hank had declared that he was heading back but that we could stay for a day more if we wanted. We'd wanted.

As soon as Uncle Hank packed his tent and left, John said, "Let's go exploring." He had a stick that he carried like a staff and he led us into the woods for a mile or so, and there it was, a small clearing and a little pond. It was perfect. The Ozarks were like that. You'd be going along, thinking that every tree looked like the other ones and it was nothing but forest and rock, but then you'd go a few feet more and take a right and there'd be a cleared spot just sitting there, like it'd been waiting for you. From the start, me and John both knew it was ours.

I took one look at it and started making plans, walking off the steps to a future cabin.

"It should face this way," John said, and later, "We'll need supplies." He started listing all these things we'd need.

"How do we get all that up here?" I asked.

"Hank knows people."

According to Hank, there was a whole community of people who lived off-grid in the Ozarks. Hank was somehow connected to them. It was an entire support system of people who weren't in anybody's census data.

Every summer we went back to that spot every chance

we could. We even brought Uncle Hank out there a couple of times. Last summer I'd camped there alone.

I kept sending John drawings of the spot and what the cabin would look like once we'd built it, because I wanted to give him something to look forward to, like a promise of what was waiting for him.

I was the one who drove him to the airport. He was going to fly to Little Rock and meet up with his platoon and from there he'd fly to Afghanistan. It was a little over an hour's drive. Instead of saying all the things we should've said to each other, we spent it playing the license plate game, the one where you called out the different states of the license plates you saw. I'd never been out of Arkansas, and other than basic training, neither had John, so cars from different places were something to get excited about. I always looked closely at the people driving them, like I expected them to look different from me.

I walked him all the way to the security gate.

"Don't let Benny talk you into coming back to work for him," he said. "You've already done one stint in Durrant. Let that be enough." He got in the security line. "Make sure you go with Aunt Linda when she visits Dad. He'll need to see you." He looked back once and smiled. "I'll see you at Hank's," he said.

The plan was that he would go straight to the cabin once he got back home, whenever that was. He gave me a small wave, telling me it was going to be okay.

It was the most scared I'd ever been, because it was the first time in my life that I'd have to navigate anything without him. I stayed in that spot even after I couldn't see him anymore. It was like I was stuck. Part of me was still the six-year-old kid in the back of that stolen car, waiting for John to tell me what to do next.

CHAPTER 3

#

One year I went dressed as my mom for Halloween. Creed wasn't big on Halloween, because of the evil spirits and demons and all that. The forty-five churches agreed that Halloween was probably the devil's holiday, so instead of Halloween parties and trick-or-treating, there were fall festivals. These festivals looked a lot like Halloween. Kids wore costumes and carried buckets for candy, but instead of trick-or-treating door to door, we had trunk-or-treating in the church parking lots. Parents would open their car trunks, fill them with candy, and decorate them all spooky like, but not too spooky. Church spooky. Bethany, Nick, and I always went to First Baptist Church's festival because they had the best games and a two-story bounce house and a cakewalk with red velvet cakes. They were my favorite. That year, Bethany dressed as

a rocker princess of her own creation and Nick wore a Trans-
formers costume we'd made out of cardboard boxes. My mom
had helped, buying yellow paint and supervising so he'd be
the perfect Bumblebee. Other kids went as superheroes and
witches and monsters. I went as a thirty-four-year-old nurse
with seafoam-green scrubs and too-big orthopedic shoes.
I'd wanted to *be* my mom.

When Bethany dropped me off after school, my mom was waiting for me in the living room. She was usually asleep when I
got home, because she worked the night shift at the hospital.
But this afternoon she was sitting straight up on the couch.
I knew she didn't slouch because slouching led to leaning
back, and once she leaned back, she was gone. She'd be asleep
in minutes. I had only a few seconds to process what could've
woken her up and why it was so important that she not risk
falling back asleep. Then I remembered Mrs. Bingham and
her curious face in the hall at school.

"You're awake?" I asked. Sometimes it was best to play
dumb.

"I got a call from Mr. Lewis earlier," she said.

I sat on the love seat across from her. She still wore her
scrubs. Sometimes when she came home, she crashed so hard
she didn't bother taking them off. She was so tired. I'd never
looked more like her.

"Yeah?" I asked.

"You were seen leaving school with Nick."

She waited for me to say something.

"You don't have anything to say?" she asked.

"I don't know what to say."

"Do you make your own rules now?" she asked. "Just do what you want?"

I still didn't know what to say.

"Is this senioritis? What's going on? Where did you go?" she asked. "I tried calling you."

I hadn't checked my phone. I looked to the floor and tried to think of lies. I'd never tell her about the barn. Not because I was afraid she wouldn't let me go back—she wasn't that kind of mom. I was scared she'd want to check it out for herself, and it was important to have spaces untouched by parents.

She motioned at my body, at the birds peeking out from under my dress and wrapping around my legs. "This is what you were up to? I thought we agreed you weren't going to let him do that anymore," she said.

"You and Dad agreed," I said softly. "I didn't."

She studied the birds. The irrational part of me hoped she'd think they were beautiful, but I could tell she saw them only as a map of all the places he'd touched me.

"I don't think you should be with him anymore."

She'd wanted to say that for a while now. I saw it in her face every time she talked about him. My parents' relationship with Nick was complicated. I knew they wanted to forbid me to see him, throw down the gauntlet, mark a line in the sand, all those things desperate parents did to keep their daughters away from wayward boys. But they were conflicted when it came to Nick. He'd been my friend since I was little. If we were the sum of our parts, then my parents had seen all of the pieces that made Nick who he was. They couldn't tease out the person he was now from the boy he used to be. And they'd loved that boy.

My dad had been Nick's one phone call the first time he was arrested. We were fifteen, and Nick was so scared. I didn't talk to him but I could hear the tone of his voice through the phone. The call came late. I couldn't make out what Nick was saying, but my dad kept saying things like, "It's going to be okay. I'll call a lawyer." He kept calling him "son." "It'll be okay, son," he said.

It wasn't okay, though. Nick had to spend two months at Durrant Juvenile Correctional Center. Once he was out, he started spending more time at my house, at my parents' request. I was surprised by this, worried my parents wouldn't want us to be friends anymore, but instead of pushing him away, they did the opposite. Maybe they thought if they could love him more, harder, closer, then he wouldn't turn out like his dad. They thought they could break the legacy. But they'd underestimated Benny's pull. The second time Nick was arrested, he was too embarrassed to call my dad for help, too scared my dad wouldn't give it.

"I've had bad shit happen to me," Nick said once, "but when your dad looks at me like he's disappointed in me, it really sucks."

I knew what he meant.

After his second arrest, Nick hardly ever came to my house anymore. When he did, he didn't talk to my dad, didn't meet his eyes. The rejection hurt my dad. I saw it in his face. Nick didn't do it to be mean. I knew he just wanted to be the first one to back away. My dad kept trying, but Nick held him at arm's length. Their relationship was never the same.

"We have tried again and again with Nick," my mom said. She closed her eyes, like just thinking about it made her tired. "But he's proven that it doesn't matter. He's made his choice about the kind of person he wants to be, and that isn't someone we want for you."

"So you're just giving up on him?" I asked.

"I don't want to." She leaned forward. "But I have to put you first. You're lucky you're not getting suspended. Because you've never done anything like this before, Mr. Lewis said this would be your one and only warning."

"What did he say about Nick?" I knew what he'd said, but I wanted her to say it out loud. "Does Nick get a warning, too? I guess not, though, since this isn't his first time to skip school."

She looked uncomfortable.

"So he's suspended?"

"That's between Mr. Lewis and Nick."

I knew he wasn't going to suspend Nick, though. Mr. Lewis used to suspend Nick. He used to have him in his office every other day, warning him, begging him to be better, but not this year. Mr. Lewis had given up on him, too. He'd pass Nick in the hall and never say anything, even if it'd been days and days since the last time Nick was there. No matter what Nick did, Mr. Lewis couldn't see him anymore. Maybe I should've felt honored that Mr. Lewis still cared about me, that I was one of the lucky ones, but I couldn't muster it.

"Maybe if people expected more of Nick, he could be more," I said.

"We all want more for Nick, but we can't do more for him than he's willing to do for himself. And we can't let his actions bring you down, too," my mom said.

"He's not bringing me down. It was my choice to leave with him. I'm the problem. He can't make me do things."

"I realize that there is a problem with you," she said, her face stern. "Your grades, for instance."

My face heated up. We were laying it all out on the table.

"Mr. Lewis said you failed your last two science tests and you didn't turn in an English paper. Since when are you that kid?"

Since two months ago. Since I started hearing and seeing things no one else heard or saw. I was in transition. I just didn't know what I was changing into.

"You're slipping, June. Since you were in elementary school, you've always been so good at managing your schoolwork. I've never had to check your homework or make sure you were turning things in on time. What's happening?"

I opened my mouth to tell her but it wouldn't come out.

She waited and waited, but when she realized I wasn't

going to say anything, she said, "You're grounded." She looked surprised that she'd said it.

I'd never been grounded before. There'd been no need. We sat there awkwardly for a second, neither one of us knowing what to do next.

"For how long?" I asked.

"I don't know. I'll talk to your dad when he gets home. We'll figure it out."

I stood.

"Give me your phone," she said. "And no watching TV in your room, and there won't be any outings with Nick in the foreseeable future."

I handed her my phone.

"And no Bethany."

It felt like being slapped. I had never imagined I could do something that warranted her taking away Bethany.

"There are consequences to your actions," she explained, standing now, too. "You can't just do what you want. We have rules. The school has rules and one of those rules is that you can't leave whenever you feel like it. You can't just decide not to turn something in and fail tests without consequences."

I tried walking away from her but she reached out and held my hand. "I know something is going on with you and you don't think I need to know about it."

Her voice sounded younger when she said it and it felt like my heart was being squeezed. We were the same height now, her eyes at the same level as mine. I couldn't escape them.

"I'm fine," I said. "Really."

"You're not fine, and it hurts my feelings that you think I don't see that."

She didn't say anything more for a moment, just looked at me, and then she reached out and swept my bangs across my face. "You're so tired, baby. The nights I'm home, I hear you in your room, pacing. I've talked to your dad but he says that you'll come to us when you're ready. But what if you're never ready?"

Maybe this was it, the moment I told her everything, that I couldn't think like I used to. I couldn't remember things I'd always known, or write English papers, or pass science tests.

I could do this. She'd always made it so easy to talk to her. Even the awkward birth-control conversation was easy with her.

Just say it, June.

The outline of her body blurred. It was a tiny glitch at first. If I hadn't been looking so hard at her, I would've missed it, but then it happened again. I tried focusing my eyes. I counted to ten. Her shadow detached from her body and moved free from her and onto the walls of the living room and my stomach slipped down to my feet.

"June?" she asked. "What's wrong?"

My mouth flooded with saliva and I covered it. I felt like I was going to throw up. It didn't take much stress to tip my scales and I watched as her shadow walked into the kitchen.

"Don't ignore me when I'm standing right in front of you. I deserve better."

She did, but I couldn't stop watching the shadow. It moved around the kitchen like it was looking for something.

I inhaled deeply through my nose. "Mama, I need to go lie down."

Her face switched from stern to concerned. She sat back down on the couch, pulling me with her, because I only called her mama when I was sick.

"I'm here," she said. "We'll just sit for a minute."

I was too old and too big to sit in her lap but I let it happen because I needed it. She ran her hand across my back and hummed, a move from my childhood. It was a nursery rhyme. When I was little, she had read to me every night before bed. The nursery rhymes were my favorites. I liked the rhythm.

We sat like that for a time, me with my eyes closed tight. Eventually the nausea passed and she stopped humming, her hand stopped moving. It took me a minute to realize she was asleep. I didn't want to move, because if I did, she'd wake up. I kept still and listened to the sound of her breathing, matching mine to hers. I picked up humming the tune where she left off. It was "Twinkle, Twinkle, Little Star."

In the dark blue sky you keep, the voice said, singing the rhyme now.

My hum died in my throat and I gripped my mom tighter.
And often through my curtains peep,
For you never shut your eye.

"June?" my mom said. I'd woken her up. "It's okay. Don't cry."

"I need to go to my room," I said. "To take a nap," I lied. "I think it'll make me feel better."

I got up and fled. She didn't stop me and she didn't follow me. She knew when to push and when not to.

I spent the evening and into the night in my bedroom, under the covers, hiding, because I was a coward. I couldn't face what was happening to me. I couldn't tell my mom the truth, even when she begged. I was worthless.

My dad came home around eight o'clock.

"She's not feeling like herself," I heard my mom explain when he asked about me. I waited for her to tell him about me skipping school and being grounded. I waited for her to tell him about what happened after, but she didn't say anything else.

He poked his head into my room when he came upstairs. I turned to him but couldn't see him, because I'd covered my eyes with my mom's compression sleep mask. I couldn't see a shadow on a wall do crazy things, like walk away from the person it belonged to, if I couldn't see anything.

"You have a headache?" he asked.

I nodded. A lie.

His footsteps were heavy as he moved to my bed, his hand on my forehead cool.

"Any fever?" he asked, always the doctor.

"No."

"Did you take something?"

"Some Tylenol earlier." Another lie.

He rubbed my head. He touched my shoulder, right where a bird was painted. I waited for him to say something about it, but instead he said, "I'm headed to bed. Come get me if it doesn't get better soon."

"Okay."

"I love you, June Bug," he said before closing my door. He sounded sad when he said it and I didn't know why.

My dad was Creed's favorite success story. He had graduated from Brown University, the only kid in Creed to go Ivy League. The plan was always to come back home, though. Go away, learn, and come back to reinvest in your community. That was what he'd been taught. He got a hero's return. There wasn't a parade, but it was close. But he brought them back something they hadn't expected. My mom. She was one of only a few people who could claim they'd move *to* Creed. She fit right in, though. It was unexpected. Maybe it was because she loved my dad so much. "He can do anything," she said to me once. "He's the smartest man I know." He was the smartest man I knew, too.

I wasn't sure how much time had passed when I heard tapping on my window. My room was on the second floor but there was a ladder that ran up the outside of the house. My parents weren't stupid and knew that I used it to sneak out sometimes, and sometimes Nick and Bethany used it to sneak in, but the worry that I'd be trapped upstairs in a fire won out over other worries.

I sat up in bed but didn't take off the mask. I treated it as a test to see how long it would take me to figure out if it was Nick or Bethany. Another part of me worried that it was neither. The window lifted, because it was never locked. There was the sound of a bag being tossed into the room and I could tell from the weight of it that it was Bethany's.

"Well, don't you look dramatic," she said.

I guessed she was referring to the mask. I pushed it up.

"Your mom called my mom," she explained, and then climbed through the window. "I can't believe you're grounded. Have you heard from Nick?"

I gave her a deadpan look.

"Oh, right, no phone. He called me earlier," she said. "But I didn't hear it and now he's not answering."

She went to my closet and started going through my clothes, like she was looking for something.

"Leanne Smith is having a party tonight," she said. "I'd wanted you to come with me, but that was before you went all troubled teen on me and got yourself grounded." She pulled out a shirt and held it up for me. "Can I borrow this?"

It was a Guns N' Roses T-shirt that I never wore, ironically.

"Yes," I said.

She pulled off her shirt, put on mine, and went to stand in front of my mirror. "I look good in this," she said.

Bethany never had a confidence problem.

"You do," I agreed.

She shoved the shirt she'd been wearing into her bag.

"What time is it?" I asked.

She fumbled around in the bag, pulling out her phone. "It is 11:45 p.m., time for all good girls to be in bed." She motioned toward me in the bed and smiled.

"I think I want to go to the party," I said.

Bethany's eyes looked like they might pop out of her head. "Who are you and what have you done with my best friend?"

She came to the bed and put her hand on my forehead in dramatic fashion. " 'I think you're a rebel,' " she said, all breathy, quoting this cheesy TV show we'd watched that was supposed to be for kids but was actually a what-to-look-for-when-your-teen-goes-bad show for parents. " 'I think you might've been one all along,' " she added.

We laughed and then she slapped her hands across her mouth and mine, like she'd just remembered that she wasn't supposed to be there. My mom had taken the night off. She'd said it was so she could catch up on sleep, but I thought she didn't want to leave me. I didn't know what would happen if she caught Bethany in my room.

"Let's do this," she said. "Go pick out something cute to wear." She flung my covers back. "And brush your teeth. I got a whiff of that breath just a second ago and it's not good."

I went to the closet, trying not to think about all the reasons this was a stupid idea. I just didn't want to stay in my room by myself and be scared anymore.

"Do we call Nick?" Bethany asked.

I shook my head. "He's working tonight."

She didn't say anything. She hated it as much as I did.

"It'll be fun to do something just the two of us," I said, trying to change the mood back.

"We're going to a party. I don't think you can count it as an outing for just the two of us."

"Do you want to do something else?"

She thought about it and then shook her head. "No, I want to do something loud."

I was dressed and climbing down the ladder fifteen minutes later. I'd brushed my teeth.

In case my parents heard the roar that was Bethany's truck cranking, she put it in neutral and we pushed it down the street a good ways before hopping in and taking off.

"It's like we've done this before," she said.

As soon as I closed the truck door, I worried that leaving was a mistake. My headache was real now.

"Are you okay?" Bethany asked.

"Yeah, just a headache."

"Are you sure this party is a good idea?"

I nodded, but I could tell she didn't believe me.

"If you change your mind when we get there, just use the bat signal and we're out of there."

The bat signal was one of us saying "I'm ready to go," but Bethany liked to pretend we had more elaborate systems.

The party was a bad idea. I knew it right after we got there, but I didn't want to admit it yet. Too many people pushing and pressing against me, moving and dancing together in the tiny living room with brown-paneled walls. I felt nauseated, the sick feeling from earlier back again. I blamed it on how hot it was in the house. I didn't look too closely at anyone, scared their shadows might do something unexpected.

June, you're slipping, the voice said.

It whispered so close to my face that I felt my hair move. Hands, arms, faces, braided above me. Mouths opened into smiles so big I was afraid they'd swallow me. My hair caught in someone's fingers, pulling my head toward them. Too close. The beer from their cup spilled down my shirt, waking up my skin. No, no, this was all wrong.

Go with it, the voice said.

The music was something I could see, painting purples and pinks across the room, and I closed my eyes. I didn't want to go with it. *Fight it,* I told myself, but my body folded into the rocking, winding bodies, pushing and pressing.

"June? What's wrong?" Bethany asked. "Are you okay?"

I was not okay. Bethany was right next to me, leaning in close. She grabbed my hands and pulled me toward her, but she wasn't strong enough to untangle me from the people in the room. She didn't stop trying. "Come on. Let's go outside," she said.

But I couldn't leave. I was a part of them now.

When she realized it was no use, she wrapped her arms around me. "It's okay," she said. We swayed to the music. "You'll be fine."

The tempo changed, the bodies shifting, pushing us toward the hall, and Bethany saw our chance.

"Let's go," she said.

The front door slammed behind us and the night air hit my face in a whoosh. It felt like being resuscitated. We skipped down the front steps of the house. The voice inside my head dulled, but then a buzzing sound began.

Buzzzzzzzzzzzzz

The buzzing was worse.

We stood on the gravel drive and Bethany stared at me for a really long time, scared of the answer to the question she wanted to ask me. *What's wrong with you, June?*

She thinks you're stupid.

It was a young girl's voice this time and I whipped my head around, trying to find her. I slammed my eyes shut and wanted to go back inside where the music made it harder to hear the goddamn voices whispering in my head.

She thinks you're the stupidest person she's ever met, the little girl said in her pretty singsong voice. I couldn't do this anymore, just grin and bear it, pretend it wasn't happening.

"Shut up," I said.

"What?" Bethany asked.

"Not you. I'm sorry." Bethany deserved a better best friend. I wanted to make her understand. "I'm slipping," I said.

"What? What does that mean?" she asked.

It was no use. I couldn't make her understand. There was no point to anything anymore.

"Where are you going?" she asked.

"I need something to drink."

I needed relief.

Shot glasses were lined up along the kitchen island and Todd Nobles poured clear liquor into them. The alcohol burned down my throat. If I was drunk enough, I could ignore the voices. Todd slow-clapped and smiled like he was proud of me, like me taking the shot was a performance.

One more bad choice, the little girl said. *You can't stop us. We'll never stop.*

Another shot and my throat was on fire. Todd cheered louder.

We will be with you forever, another one said. *Always listening.*

Three shots. Maybe I could burn the voices down.

Always whispering in your ear. You'll never be alone, they said together.

"June, stop," Bethany said. Her hands were on me, taking the glass from my hand.

"Where's the bathroom?" I asked.

This felt like dying.

"I think there's one upstairs. If you don't feel good, we can just go." She said it like she was desperate for us to go.

I took the stairs two at a time. "I just need a minute."

Maybe this was an anxiety attack. My mom had them sometimes. She said they felt like dying.

The bathroom was decorated in turquoise and hot pink, two colors that should never go together. I risked a look in the mirror. It was worse than I thought. My face told the truth.

There's no hiding anymore, the voices said. *Everyone will look at you and know. They'll know you're crazy.*

"Shut. Up."

You're crazy. Crazy. Crazy.

How to make it stop? Louder, it needed to be louder, louder than the music from downstairs and the voices from inside. If I couldn't drown out the voices, I would die on this turquoise bath mat. The sound of water would help. I turned the water on in the sink, full force, but it wasn't loud enough. I went to the shower. I couldn't turn the water on, couldn't make it work. It wasn't like ones I'd used before. Stupid Leanne Smith had a faucet I'd never seen before.

I hated crying. Crying was quitting. Stop crying. Stop crying. Thank God the water came on. Relief. More, louder, yes. The shower would help drown out the noise.

My head pounded. It felt like something was stuck inside me and was trying to get out. Distracting myself, I counted the tiles on the floor. I'd feel better once I knew exactly how many tiles were in this bathroom. One, two, three, four. They were like the cracks in the sidewalk on the way to school. Five, six, seven.

I was going to die if whatever was in my head didn't get out.

Eight, nine, ten.

It had to get out.

My fingernails tore through the skin on my face so easily. I thought it'd be harder. It should hurt but I couldn't feel anything. I watched my face in the mirror, my skin curling in places, reminding me of a potato peeling. Why didn't it hurt?

Because you are not a real person, the voices answered.

"June?" It was Bethany. She tried the handle, but I'd locked the door. "We've got to go. Now. We're busted. Your mom is calling my phone."

What would I do when my mom came for me, because Bethany was going to answer that phone. I'd gone too far this time. Bethany was scared. I had seen it in her eyes when we were outside.

How was I supposed to look when I tried to convince my mom I wasn't insane? Stand this way? I practiced how I'd stand but I didn't know where to put my hands. Where would I put my shaking hands that told the truth?

It's an anxiety attack, I'd tell her. *You have them, so I have them. That explains it. We're two peas in a pod. You've always said so.*

I'd hide my hands in my pockets and stand just this way when she came. Maybe I'd smile and it wouldn't be a scary one, but a sure smile. I was sure. She'd think I was fine.

Someone pounded on the door.

No, no. I wasn't ready. I needed more time to practice my normal face. My smile was still scary. My face still bled.

More pounding.

"June? I swear to God, if you don't let me know you're okay, I'm busting the door down."

Nick. Bethany had called Nick. It wasn't my mom to take me away, but Nick, who would help me keep my secret a little longer.

"Let me in," he said.

I wanted to answer him but my voice died in my throat.

"June?" he said.

There were thirty-five tiles in the bathroom. I was sure. I wasn't sure of anything else, but I knew how many tiles were on the floor. I'd counted them over and over. There were three steps to the door. The knob was cold in my hand but I couldn't open it.

"I told Benny I was quitting," he said.

He said it in a whisper, like he worried someone else might hear.

"Really?" I asked.

"Yeah," he said. "I'm trying."

He was trying to be different. He was going to quit Benny's. It was what I'd wanted since he'd started working there. I wanted to feel happy about it. I wanted to feel anything but the splitting of my head.

"Can I come in?" he asked.

"No," I said. "Not yet."

"Why not?"

"Not right now," I said. Not like this. We'd never be able to pretend I was okay if he saw me like this.

"It's all right," he said. "I'm not scared."

But he should be.

"They won't shut up. They keep talking and I can't *think*."

He was quiet for a long moment and I gripped the doorknob harder.

"They're not real," he said finally.

"They sound real."

"I know," he said, "but they're not."

"I don't know what's real."

"You do. I'm real. Focus on *my* voice. I'm real, June."

He was right. There was no one more real than him.

"Do you believe me?" he asked. He did sound scared now. "I know you know I'm real. Tell me what you know."

Pressing my forehead against the door, I said, "I know you're real."

"Yes," he said, relieved. "Tell me what else you know."

"I know that we have plans this summer."

"What are they?" he asked.

"We're going to see your uncle, and John will be there."

"Yes."

"You're going to show me where you and John camp."

"Yes," he repeated.

"It's going to be perfect," I said.

Nick had told me about the shade of purple he'd seen only when the sun rose over the Ozarks and I was going to see it and it would be perfect. Maybe the voices wouldn't follow me to the mountains.

We will be in the mountains, they said, and tears fell.

"I can't promise perfect," he said. "But it'll be better because you'll be there. Now, either you come out of the bathroom or let me in. Please."

Nick rarely begged.

"Okay," I said.

I turned off the water in the shower and sink. I smoothed my hair.

It didn't help.

There was too much evidence of all that was wrong with me and not enough time to hide it all.

I opened the door.

"Damn, June," Nick said, his hands going to my face. "What did you do? You look like you've been in a fight."

I had been.

"I can't hold it back anymore," I said.

I thought I'd have to explain but he nodded. He understood. We'd been holding it back together, the three of us. Bethany stood next to him, her face a mixture of concern and fear. She had bags under her eyes. How long had they been there? How long had my problems been taking a toll on her, too?

Bethany noticed my tears and she started crying. "You'll never cry alone if I'm in the room," she'd said to me once. Our tears wouldn't stop. The dam had broken and we were all going to drown.

"Let's get out of here," Nick said.

We walked back through the house, a train with me in the middle. They held my hands and Nick led us. It was the same way we'd walk through any crowd. It didn't matter if we got lost, as long as we didn't lose each other.

We were in Nick's car, knee to knee. Bethany still held my hand.

I felt better in the car, away from the party and all the noise and the heat from all those bodies. It was safer here. I could breathe.

"Let's go to the barn," I said, too scared to go home right away. "We can use the lamps that your dad gave us," I said to Bethany.

Her dad owned the hardware store and he'd given me and Bethany these battery-powered lamps for when we camped in our backyards.

She didn't say anything, though, just squeezed my hand tighter in hers. Her eyes held apologies and I didn't know why.

"It's going to be okay," I told both of them. "I'm feeling much better now."

They didn't look convinced and we rode in silence. Bethany's phone rang. I was sure it was my mom.

"I know I'm in trouble," I said. "I'm in more trouble than I've ever been in."

Bethany silenced her phone.

"But that's exactly why we need to go to the barn. You can't take me home right now."

My parents couldn't see me like this.

"I need more time to get myself together and my parents are probably seconds away from calling the police. Once they get their hands on me, y'all may never see me again. We should make the most of tonight. Let's go to the barn," I pleaded.

Nick's phone rang.

"Don't answer it," I said.

I wouldn't put it past my parents to lock me away in my room, Rapunzel-style. They'd take away the ladder this time.

"You're going the wrong way," I said to Nick. "We should've turned back there."

It was rare that I knew where to go and he didn't. He acted like he didn't hear me.

"Nick?"

We rode in silence and I thought about how many times we'd ridden in Nick's car just like this. We always sat three in the front seat, because it never felt right to put Bethany in the back.

The car pulled to a stop in front of my house. Nick put it in park and Bethany started crying again. Now I knew why she was sorry.

My face heated up. "When y'all said you'd never tell, you were lying?" It hurt to swallow. My hands shook again. "When you said you'd help me. Those were lies?" I asked again.

Neither one of them would look me in the eyes.

"This is how we help you," Nick said, staring straight ahead.

We sat there for a while before anybody moved. It took a few minutes to digest broken promises.

"What time is it?" I asked Nick.

The clock on his dash had been broken for a while, so

he leaned forward and pulled his phone out of his pocket. "2:17," he said.

2:17.

I wiped my eyes.

It was time to tell the secret.

CHAPTER 4

There were things I knew for sure. There were three bedrooms in my house. It was a two-story house with seventeen steps on the stairs. My house had six plants in it, all in different stages of dying because my mom couldn't keep plants alive and my dad wasn't aware we had plants. My backyard had a trampoline I hadn't jumped on in two years and next to it was a doghouse that had never had a dog in it, because we couldn't decide which kind we wanted. It took twenty-six of my steps to get from Nick's car to my front door. Nick and Bethany would never leave my side. My front door was heavy and wooden and made the exact same noise every time it opened, like it was exhausted from opening. My parents would be standing in the kitchen. They loved me. These were the things I knew for sure.

They were standing in the kitchen. From the looks on their faces, their worry and fear outweighed their anger. Nick and Bethany were at my side.

"June, oh my God, where did you go, what happened to you, what happened to your face, I can't believe you let us worry like this, where did you go, where were you, have you been drinking, how much have you had to drink, are you okay, are you okay, are you okay?"

Their questions tumbled out of their mouths and rolled over me. There were too many to answer, so I focused on the last one.

"I'm not okay," I admitted.

My mom's hand was on my face now, turning it toward the light, examining the scratches. She moved me so slowly, checking me over, her movements cautious, like I was a bomb that might go off in her kitchen.

"Explain," my dad said. He looked between all of us, finally landing on Nick. My dad looked resigned and a little sad, like he was pretty sure that whatever was going on was Nick's fault but he really didn't want it to be.

"Something is wrong," I said.

"What's wrong?" he asked, still looking only at Nick.

I pulled away from my mom and stepped in front of Nick so my dad would have to see me. "Something is wrong with me," I said.

He looked at me, distracted.

"I think I'm sick," I said.

His eyes changed. I saw the switch, because I knew to look for it. He transformed from dad to doctor.

"What do you mean?" he asked, his hand on my forehead again.

"Not that kind of sick," I said.

My mom pulled out a kitchen chair and motioned for me to sit in it. I plopped down, grateful for the invitation. I couldn't face this standing.

I thought of the words I needed to explain this. I'd practiced saying them. I'd written them down in my notebook. It went like this . . . It went like this . . . My mouth opened. It went like this.

Nothing.

"Someone had better start talking," my mom said.

"I can't think anymore," I blurted out.

"She gets lost all the time," Bethany said.

"She doesn't sleep," Nick added quietly, from his spot by the door.

Bethany stepped closer to my mom. "She's sick," she said.

It sounded like a train coming, the whistle sound of metal on metal coming faster and faster toward us. The noise was piercing and I clamped my hands over my ears. It was so high-pitched that it hurt my teeth, my jaw locking, making me choke on my scream. I whipped my head around, trying to find the source of the noise, and then I remembered that a tornado can sound like a train. We needed to get to the hall or a bathtub. I tried moving, but the tornado affected the gravity inside my house, because my legs didn't work.

Twenty-five tornadoes hit Arkansas last year.

Twenty-five tornadoes hit Arkansas last year.

Twenty-five. Tornadoes. Hit Arkansas. Last year.

My jaw unlocked with an audible pop. No one ran, even though I screamed and screamed for them to do so, my voice burning from my throat, burning, burning.

"June!" I heard someone yell, my mom maybe.

Their hands were on me, holding me, and I slammed my eyes shut. We had to hide. But it was too late. We couldn't hide from this.

The tornado must have hit the house, because there was the sound of wood splintering, glass shattering, like an explosion, splitting me down the middle, and I died.

CHAPTER 5

There was only one thing that June had asked us to do for her that was important.

"Don't tell," she'd said. "Please," she'd begged.

When she said it, she had the same look on her face that John had had when he'd wanted me to understand why he was leaving. It didn't matter that I didn't understand or that the idea scared me. I wanted to make her happy.

"I don't need anyone else's help," she said to me and Bethany.

I didn't know about Bethany, but when June said that, I felt like I was twelve feet tall. I knew she wasn't just saying it to get us to do what she wanted. June wasn't like that. She really thought we were all she needed.

I liked being what she needed. I loved it. We thought that

we could handle it, that it was some weird phase and it would go away and she'd be fine. We had no idea it would lead us here. To this moment. And I still didn't know if we'd done the right thing. Even if we had, I had done the one thing I'd promised I would never do, and now she might not ever forgive me.

We were following her parents in their car. Bethany rode with me. I'd helped June's dad carry June to their car. It was a two-person job, because June fought us like her life depended on it, like she thought we were trying to hurt her. My face burned and bled from her scratches. Her mom said we should wait for an ambulance, but her dad wasn't hearing it.

"No," he said. "We're not waiting."

Her mom got in the back seat with her so she could hold her. June kept screaming and screaming and I didn't know what she was saying and then she went quiet. She folded in on herself like a deflated balloon. The quiet was worse than the screaming. Her dad even checked her pulse. June stared straight ahead, not responding.

I'd never seen her dad scared before. This was a man who always had the answers.

We were almost there. Bethany had been talking nonstop but only saying five words. Over and over, she kept saying, "She's going to be okay. She's going to be okay. She's going to be okay."

CHAPTER 6

JUNE

I woke up in the hospital in Creed. I'd know this hospital anywhere, because I'd spent my childhood playing in its halls. A nurse was in the room with me and her name was Dorothy. She was friends with my mom. My mom called her Dot, all of her friends did, and her grandkids called her Dottie. She used to bring them to my birthday parties. "Dottie, they have a trampoline. Can we jump on it?" they'd ask. Dottie had always said yes.

She looked at me sweetly. She looked at me like she looked at the babies in the nursery. I was confused, because I was sure I'd died and I was not a baby.

"It's good to see you awake," she said.

They must've resuscitated me, sewed me back together. I flung the sheet off myself and looked under my gown for any evidence of this, but there wasn't any.

"Don't get upset, baby," she cooed.

"I'm not a baby," I said.

"Be still," she said, covering me back up. "You've had a rough go of it. You still need to rest."

"There was a tornado," I said. "It hit my house. Is everyone else okay? Where are my parents? Have you seen them?"

Where were Nick and Bethany?

"There wasn't a tornado," Dot said, her face a picture of calm.

"There was. It hit my house. It was bad." My voice shook.

"Shhhh. It's okay," she said. "Don't cry."

She tried to hold me, her fingers cold on my arms.

"Please stop," I said, pushing her away. "I'm not crazy. There was a tornado. Can you get my dad or my mom? Where are they?"

"You calm down and I'll go get them. They haven't been home since you were admitted."

"How many people died?" I asked, but she was already walking out of the room. "How many people died?!" I screamed.

She didn't come back with my parents but with another nurse and a big man. His name tag said CURTIS.

"Where are my parents?"

"They're on their way. We're going to need you to stay calm, though. Mrs. Odom is going to give you something to relax you."

"I don't need to be relaxed. This is no time to be relaxed."

They didn't listen, their hands on me, holding me down.

"Please stop. You need to call the police, or the National Guard."

People needed help.

"No," I said. "Don't do this. I don't want to be calm right now. Where's my dad?"

The needle pricked my skin and burned into my veins.

"No!" I screamed. "No, no, no!" I'd never screamed at adults before. "I need my dad!"

And then I heard him. "It's okay, June Bug," he said, out of breath, his voice right next to my ear. "The medicine will help you rest. You're going to be okay."

I couldn't keep my eyes open. Whatever they had given me worked fast. "There was a tornado," I said.

"Those won't be necessary," my mom said. She was here now, too. "Steve, tell them not to use them."

"Those won't be necessary," my dad said to someone else, his voice stern. "No, we won't need them. I'll stay with her. It's okay," he said to me.

He rubbed my arm and I concentrated on the feel of it.

"It's okay. I'm with you," he said. "I'm with you. I'm with you," he kept saying.

I wished I could see him. I'd never heard him cry before.

There was no tornado. My parents showed me pictures of our house with the date on them and my house stood just as it always did, looking like it always did. There should have been a gaping hole down the middle that had ripped through the kitchen, but there was no hole, no rip, nothing.

The tornado was me.

My dad ran every test imaginable on me, trying to find something to explain what was happening. I was a problem he had to solve. It killed him that he didn't know what was wrong with me. I saw it in his eyes every time he came to check on me. He was a doctor, so he felt like he should've realized something was wrong.

When my CAT scan came back normal, I thought he was actually disappointed. Not that he wanted me to have a tumor or anything, but I knew it'd make him feel better if whatever was going on was something he could point to on a scan.

"See, right here," he'd say, and point. "This is the problem."

He'd pulled some strings and gotten a doctor to come down from Little Rock. They'd gone to medical school together. Everyone kept calling her a specialist instead of a psychiatrist, but I was pretty sure she was a psychiatrist. I didn't know why they were hiding that word from me. If the problem wasn't physical, then it had to be mental.

I had permission to tell her everything.

"Be honest with her," my mom had said. "Unburden yourself. She can't help you if she doesn't know everything."

Maybe it'd be good to tell someone everything.

The night before she came, I'd been moved to the fourth floor of the hospital. I'd never been on that floor. You had to have a special key to a special elevator to get to the fourth floor. None of the other elevators in the hospital stopped there. Their numbers skipped right over it: 1, 2, 3, 5. This had intrigued me when I was little and visited my parents at work.

"Where do they keep the fourth floor?" I'd asked my mom.

"Right above the third floor."

I hadn't believed her, though. I hadn't believed it could be that simple. I was sure that they were hiding it, that it was like something out of *Alice in Wonderland*. I imagined a sideways fourth floor with doors that opened out instead of in and people who walked on ceilings. The nurses wore uniforms with purple stripes and all the medicine was candy. There were no shots.

To say that the actual fourth floor was a disappointment was an understatement. I knew I shouldn't have been so excited, but I'd held my breath when I'd stepped off the elevator, just in case. There was something special in seeing something that not everyone else was allowed to see. It looked like all the other floors, though. The nurses wore regular scrubs, and not even in fun colors. There were shots, and I got one.

"To help you sleep," the nurse had said.

Now I was in a tiny room with white furniture and white walls. The chair I sat in was made of vinyl and was cold, making me cold. I was waiting to see the specialist, and I was right. She was a psychiatrist. She worked at Little Rock Psychiatric Hospital. It turned out the fourth floor was the mental health ward. The secret elevator was so not just anyone could waltz in. "To protect confidentiality," a nurse had said. My parents were joining us later. They thought it would be a good idea to meet with her by myself first.

My dad had told me the psychiatrist's name was Dr. Keels and she was the best he knew about, the best around. It'd probably made the resident psychiatrist mad that he brought her in, but my dad didn't care who he hurt when it came to helping me. We were lucky to have the resources that we had in a town as small as Creed. Other towns our size might have hospitals but most of them didn't have psychiatric wards. It was because we were so far from anything that resembled a city. We were more than a hundred miles from the next hospital. People from all around used Creed's hospital, not just the people who lived here, so it came with a few bells and whistles that other small-town hospitals didn't have.

I wasn't left alone to wait. I'd learned in the short time I'd been there that privacy wasn't a luxury you got to keep on this floor. The nurse with me was named Janet and she'd grown up in Creed. She had just graduated and this was her first real job. We'd gotten to know each other in the past twenty-four hours. It felt right that I should ask her questions about herself. I needed to know something about her since I had to pee in front of her.

The door pushed open and a woman swept into the room like a wave. She wore red from head to toe. She had red hair and red lipstick and a red pantsuit that she had to have sewed herself, because there couldn't be much demand for red pant-suits. Her earrings were strawberries and I worried she might not be real, so I looked to Nurse Janet for confirmation and she nodded, like *Yes, this is who you've been waiting for.* Then I remembered that she was a child psychiatrist. Maybe this was her "relatable" outfit. She reminded me of a character from a picture book. I couldn't remember the name, but I was pretty sure I liked it.

She shut the door and sat in the seat across from me, the smell of her perfume wafting toward me. She smelled like honeysuckle and I was disappointed, because it should've been strawberry.

"Hi, June," she said.

I waved. It was a weird thing to do, but I felt pretty weird.

"Janet, would you mind giving us some privacy?"

Janet nodded and walked out of the room, but before she shut the door she met my eyes and smiled. I'd miss her.

Dr. Keels looked down at the notepad in her hands. "I like your name. I've not met many Junes."

She said it like she'd met a lot of Aprils and Mays.

"It was my grandmother's name," I explained.

"That's nice. I've always liked the tradition of handing down names."

I had, too.

"Your dad gave me an idea of what's been going on, but I'd like to hear it from you."

I didn't know what she wanted me to say, how I should

start. If this was a TV show, I'd be lying down on a couch or staring out a window into the middle distance, but this was real life and this room didn't have a couch or a window. I didn't know what to say and I didn't know where to look.

"It's okay, June," she said, like she could read my mind. "This can go however you want it to." She tilted her head to the side, like she was thinking of something for the first time. "Do you have an idea of how you'd like it to go?"

"Not any good ones," I said. "I'd just like to be honest."

"I'd appreciate your honesty."

I slid my hands underneath my legs to keep them still. I was nervous. "If it's okay with you, I'd like to pretend that I'm just a person and you're just a person and we're having a conversation and nothing is weird and we didn't just meet and there's no high stakes. We're just talking."

She leaned in and I tried not to be distracted by the sound of the red fabric rubbing against her legs. It sounded like polyester.

"We are just people and we're just talking," she said. "There are no high stakes and nothing is weird." She put down her notebook. "My name is Brooke. I've known your parents for a long time. Your dad has been trying to get me to come down from Little Rock for a while now."

"He said you met in med school."

She nodded. "We were partners in anatomy class."

"Was he a good partner?"

"The best. He was always very organized. He took excellent notes. People offered to pay him for them."

That didn't surprise me. He was meticulous, like me. It was another reason he couldn't forgive himself for not seeing what was in front of him.

"Your dad says you're good at taking notes, too." She pointed at my notebook on the coffee table between us. When I'd told my dad that I'd written everything down, he'd brought it to me and encouraged me to share it with Dr. Keels.

"I write down everything," I admitted.

"Like a diary?"

I shrugged. "Sort of."

"What types of things do you write in it?"

"There are different sections for different things. I've been keeping one for a while now. This is my second one this year."

"Your dad mentioned that you had more than one."

"Mm-hmm."

They all looked the same, though. Blue five-subject notebooks with college-ruled paper that I kept on a shelf in my room.

"Why do you think you keep them?" she asked.

I thought about it. "I'm an observer. I notice things, things maybe other people don't, or just things I need to remember, so I write it all down so there's a record. I like having a record."

"Did you write about the things you've been experiencing?"

"Yes."

"Can you tell me about some of them?"

It was weird to go from admitting something was wrong

to my parents to saying it to a stranger. It was too personal. I didn't know her.

"What's your favorite color?" I asked.

She looked confused at first but then said, "Today it's red."

"Today?"

She nodded. "My favorite color depends on the day. When I woke up today, I was feeling red." She waved her arm across her body.

I smiled. "I want to imagine that your closet is full of monochromatic pantsuits. Please don't tell me I'm wrong."

"You're not far off the mark," she said.

"Did you always want to be a psychiatrist?" I asked.

"Yes."

"Why?"

"I've always wanted to help people."

"You had to go to school for a long time for that. Longer than my dad did. Are your parents proud?"

"I think if they were still alive, they would be," she said.

"I'm sorry."

"It's okay. It happened a long time ago. A car accident," she said.

"I'm sorry," I said again. It didn't matter that she'd said it was okay.

"Can we play a game?" she asked.

"Do you get to make the rules?"

"Yes," she said without apology.

"Do I have a choice?"

"With me, you always have a choice."

"Okay, then. Let's play."

"Pretend that I'm not here."

"You're kind of hard to ignore. What with all that red."

I was deflecting. She knew it.

She smiled. "Close your eyes."

I closed them.

"Take a deep breath and pretend you're in the room alone."

But that was impossible.

"I'm never alone," I said.

"Why are you never alone?"

Because the things I couldn't control were living in my head with me, like parasites.

"There's a lot of noise in my head."

"Can you tell me about the noise?"

It was hard to describe. It wasn't always voices or distinct sounds. Sometimes it was a low hum, this constant background noise. I didn't know how long it'd been there. With my eyes still closed, I tried to hear it so I could describe it to her, but it never happened on command.

"I don't know how," I said.

"Could you try?" she asked. "Or maybe it would be easier if you read something to me from your notebook."

I opened my eyes. Would that be easier?

"Or I could read something from it," she said. "If you'd prefer."

The idea scared and excited me at the same time. I opened

the notebook to the right section and handed it to her. She'd be the first person to read it besides me. She began reading, and a few seconds later she frowned, her brows furrowing.

"This is in third person," she said.

I nodded. I never wrote it like it was happening to me, always *she* or *her,* never *me.*

"'There is something inside of her trying to get out,'" Dr. Keels read. "'Like an animal clawing. The pain is so real that she checks her body, looking for marks. She keeps her mouth closed most of the time, because she's scared if she doesn't, it will escape.'"

My days were spent with muscles coiled tight, mouth pressed tight. I couldn't afford to relax. I didn't know what would happen if it got out.

"What do you think is trying to get out?" she asked.

"I don't know," I said.

"How does that make you feel?" she asked.

Like I was choking on all the things I couldn't say. I shrugged.

She kept reading. "'She never sleeps.'" She looked up at me. "When did you start having trouble sleeping?"

"A couple of months ago."

"How long did you go without sleep?"

Days and days and days.

"A while."

I knew that I had slept some, because I'd wake up occasionally, so I must've gone to sleep at some point.

"There's too much to think about, worry about," I said. "During the day, I worry less, because there are so many distractions, but at night there's nothing else to do but lie there and I can't turn off my mind and it just runs and runs."

My thoughts chased each other until they merged into one constant stream.

"Did something occur during that time that could trigger not being able to sleep? Anything stressful or traumatic?"

That was when Bethany and I had started hearing back from colleges, nothing most people would think was traumatic. Letters came every day, telling us, "Congratulations!" or "We regret to inform you . . ." We didn't always get into the same places. I'd stay up late, reading everything about the ones that had said yes to both of us, where they were and what their cities had to offer us. I'd take notes, cataloging everything. I was so worried about choosing the right one, about not being able to bring Nick along. The future terrified me. Bethany seemed to take it all in stride. "Don't stress, June," she'd say. But it wasn't a choice for me.

"We started getting acceptance and rejection letters from different universities," I said.

"We?"

"My best friend, Bethany, and me. We'd get mail every day. I started worrying over them. I like to have a plan. I want to know what's coming, you know, what to expect. There was too much to think about and not enough day to do it, so I made myself stay awake until I knew everything about whatever school we'd heard from that day, and not just the school but the place."

I had an entire notebook full of facts about each university.

"Not sleeping was a choice," I said. "At first."

"But over time you developed insomnia," she said.

"I guess."

She flipped through my notebook. I felt a little queasy. I didn't just write down observations. Some of my most private thoughts were in there.

"You've time-stamped some things," she said.

"I wanted to see if I could establish a pattern."

"You're very smart, June. I think you'd make a good scientist."

"My science teacher would disagree."

"I think your science teacher knows you're smart, too. What's this?" she asked. She turned the notebook so I could see. "Why the quotation marks?"

"They're things I heard," I said. My voice was squeaky and I hated it.

"Who said them?"

"I never named them."

"Are you hearing voices?" she asked.

She asked it like it was any other question. *What do you like on your pizza?* I wanted to go back to talking about favorite colors and dead parents.

I nodded. I didn't want to admit it out loud to her yet.

"When did you start hearing them?" she asked.

"I think it was a couple of months ago."

It was hard to know exactly when it had started. For a long time, I didn't know that what I heard was something other people couldn't hear.

"About the same time you started having trouble sleeping?" she asked.

"I think so. It wasn't voices at first," I admitted.

"Can you tell me about it?"

I liked that she kept using the word *can*, like she understood that what she was asking might be something I wasn't able to do.

"At first it was sounds I could explain away, something I could rationalize. Like the doorbell ringing when I blow-dried my hair, or soft music playing in the other room, or phones ringing, things like that. I didn't know other people couldn't hear it, too. But one day my mom was home and the doorbell kept ringing over and over and I kept answering the door and no one was ever there. I thought there was a malfunction or something, like maybe there was something wrong with the wiring. She'd been asleep, because she works the night shift here at the hospital. She woke up, angry, and I thought it was because of the doorbell. But it turned out she hadn't heard the doorbell, just me opening and closing the door over and over."

I shifted in my seat.

"The first time it was a voice, I didn't take it so well."

"What did the voice say?" Dr. Keels asked.

"She sang to me."

"What did she sing?"

It was a song my mom had sung to me when I was a baby. "A lullaby called 'All Through the Night.' Do you know that one?"

"I don't," she said.

"It's really beautiful. It's about guardian angels watching over the baby as she sleeps. They stay with her through the night, protecting her."

"And the voice sang this to you?"

"Yes, she tried to sing me to sleep."

"Where did the voice come from? Did it sound like it was someone speaking in the room with you, like how I'm speaking to you now?"

I shook my head. "It came from inside me."

"What did you do when it happened?"

I'd been alone in my room. It was the middle of the night.

"I tried to get away from her. I ran to my bathroom, but she was in there, too."

I'd gone into every room of my house, but she was everywhere. I'd stood right outside my parents' bedroom door, my hand reaching for the doorknob, but then she stopped.

"I thought it was exhaustion, or my imagination, or some combination of the two, because what else could it be?"

"How often did you hear her after that?"

"Just from time to time. Whenever I was really tired, or stressed about something. And then there were more. Different voices, some older, some younger, always female."

"Did they sing, too?"

I shook my head. "They say all kinds of things."

"What kinds of things?"

"They say all the things I think about myself, my worries, my fears."

All of my insecurities, spoken to me by voices with no bodies.

"I try to ignore it. I'd gotten pretty good at ignoring them. Writing down what they said made me feel better."

It was harder to know when they were talking when I was in a room with a lot of people. I'd gotten in the habit of watching people's mouths to see if I could match the voices I heard to anyone in the room. That was another reason I liked to spend most of my time with just Nick and Bethany. It was easier to know when I was hearing voices that didn't belong to them.

"Are they ever commanding?" Dr. Keels asked.

"They don't tell me to do things, if that's what you're asking."

She scribbled on her pad.

"Are you having other symptoms besides not sleeping and the voices?" she asked.

"Like what?" I asked.

"Are you experiencing anything else unusual? Things you think other people aren't experiencing?"

"I saw my mom's shadow detach from her body and walk into the kitchen. Does that count?"

"Yes," she said, back to scribbling.

"And one day I thought I saw my friend Becky. She was standing on Walton Street where we used to meet to walk to school together."

"That's not unusual, is it?"

"She's been missing for more than a year. I yelled out for her but she didn't hear me, because she turned and went the wrong way, back toward her house. I started running, to catch up to her."

My hands were red from wringing.

"When I got to her house, I saw her walk behind it, but when I went back there, she was gone. There was no one there. I yelled and yelled. There's a pond behind her house and for a second I thought maybe she'd gone into it."

I didn't want to talk about this anymore. It hurt to remember.

"What do you think is wrong with me?" I asked.

She looked up from her notepad. "We're trying to figure out what's going on."

"But you said *symptoms*. You asked me what other symptoms I had, so you must think that it's symptoms of something. I know you talked to my dad. He told you everything."

As if on cue, there was a knock on the door and Janet was back with my parents in tow.

Dr. Keels nodded for them to sit next to me.

"June and I were just getting to know each other," she said.

My dad was all business, shaking her hand before taking a

seat. My mom let out her breath when she saw me, like she'd been holding it for a long time. She scooted her chair closer to me.

"June has been telling me about the things she's experiencing," Dr. Keels said to them. They stared so intently at her face, like they expected to find answers there. My mom leaned forward in her chair.

"June, would you mind if I shared with your parents the things you've told me?" Dr. Keels asked.

"I don't mind."

"It appears that June has experienced some periods of psychosis." She looked each of us in the eyes one at a time, to make sure we were all paying attention. "There are a few things that can cause such episodes," she said. "I was just telling June that we're trying to figure out what may have caused hers. In order to do so, we have to rule out the possible causes until we land on one that is the most likely. All of your tests came back normal," she said to me. "Your drug screen came back normal, too."

She saw the surprise in my face. I didn't know I'd been screened for drugs.

"It's normal procedure to determine if you've taken anything psychotropic that might be causing these symptoms."

I had smoked weed once at a party in Brad Henderson's backyard, and I had taken some of Nick's aunt Linda's sleeping pills that had made me wake up feeling like my brain was full of cotton, but nothing else.

"I'll establish a working diagnosis and we'll proceed from

there, but we can go ahead and treat your symptoms and make adjustments as needed."

"What's your working diagnosis?" It was my dad.

"It's too soon to assign names. The first thing we want to do is help June establish normal sleep patterns." She looked at me. "Regular sleep is crucial to your mental health. Exhaustion from lack of sleep can cause hallucinations."

"Could that be it?" I asked. "Could I just be tired?"

"Possibly, but sometimes not being able to sleep is a symptom of something else."

"Like what?" my mom asked.

"We're not assigning any names yet," Dr. Keels reminded her.

"But if you had to give it a name? Today, right now. What would you call it?" It was my dad again. He stood now. He wore his demanding face, his I'm-ready-to-fix-this-problem face.

"Steve . . . ," my mom said.

Dr. Keels looked like she was weighing her options. She opened the bag she had come in with and pulled out pamphlets, passing them out to us.

"This is some background information that you all might want to read." She rambled on, words rolling off her tongue as she laid out the information. "There are mental illnesses that can cause symptoms like you've described." She used words like *bipolar disorder, schizophrenia, schizoaffective disorder, major depressive disorder.*

My mom put her head in her hands like she was devastated, like someone had told her I died.

Dr. Keels leaned closer to me. "The fact that no one in your family has ever reported experiencing periods of psychosis makes a good prognosis more likely," she said. She looked to my parents for confirmation and they both nodded. "It's also a good sign that you're aware that something is wrong. People who are aware that what they're experiencing is abnormal respond much better to treatment. The technical term is *insight*."

I had insight into what was wrong with me. I just didn't know what it was called yet. And neither did she.

"So what do we do about it?" I asked.

"Since being admitted, you've been given small doses of an antipsychotic. Initially it makes you sleepy, which is why you've been taking it at night. But it's not a sleeping pill. Over time that effect will wear off, so we'll introduce a sleep aid, just until you can develop normal sleep patterns on your own."

"But I'll keep taking the other one, too?"

"Yes," she said. "And we'll continue to monitor you and treat any symptoms as they come up."

"How long will I be in the hospital?" I asked.

"At least until a working diagnosis can be made. It really varies from person to person. We'll need to regulate the medications, tweak the dosages as needed. I'll need to observe you and we'll continue to chat. In the meantime, the medication has helped a lot of people with symptoms similar to yours. It can help you think more clearly, slow down those racing thoughts, help you remain able to discern reality from not."

"Will it get rid of the voices?" I asked.

"The antipsychotic likely won't reach peak effect until about three to four weeks after starting it, so you may still experience some symptoms until that time."

She must have seen the panic in my eyes, because she continued. "But you should feel the calming effect immediately. So while you may still hear voices or see things, the drug will impact how you react to them."

"They'll be less scary?"

"I hope so," she said.

"So in a few weeks, they'll be gone? It'll fix them?"

My dad leaned forward, waiting. It might have been the first time he was in a room with someone who knew more than he did about something.

"This can be a waiting game, June, and it's important to understand that a lot of these illnesses are lifelong conditions, and so is the treatment. But many people live full, independent lives. You can read about some of them in the literature I've given you. You had a psychotic episode, but that doesn't mean you can't recover from it."

"Lifelong?" I asked. It felt like my throat was closing.

"Yes," she said. "Like a lot of illnesses."

I'd woken up something inside me that was never going back to sleep.

"Think of it like asthma," she said. "Your dad has asthma. I remember from med school. He had an asthma attack one semester. He said it was the first one he'd had since he was a child."

This was true. He'd told me stories of rushed car trips to the emergency room, with the windows down so the wind in his face would keep him awake, all because he'd gotten too close to the neighbor's cat. He'd been worried I'd have similar problems, but I never did.

"If he takes his medication and avoids those things that trigger an attack, he's less likely to have one," Dr. Keels said. "It doesn't mean he won't ever have another one, but he knows what to do when he does and then he recovers from them. I don't want to oversimplify it, but I think the analogy could help explain things a bit in terms of this being an illness we can treat."

My dad avoided cats at all costs and never went anywhere without his inhaler.

"But there's no inhaler for this," I said.

What would I use to help me breathe?

"You'll have medication and me, or someone like me. You'll have other coping strategies to help you. You've already developed at least one."

She saw the confusion in my face.

"Your notebook," she said. "Writing down what happened, how it made you feel, helped you. Right?"

I nodded.

"And you have a good support system in your parents. Those things will be vital to establishing successful recovery strategies. Before, you were coping the best you could, with the tools you had. My goal is to diagnose you and help you build more tools."

"So what do we do now?" I asked.

"We watch and wait and we adjust the treatment accordingly."

CHAPTER 7

My dad hardly ever told my mom that he loved her. It wasn't that he didn't love her. He was just never comfortable with that word in the room. She stopped saying it after a while, too. Maybe because he almost never said it back. She pulled away from him a little more every day. I didn't know when he noticed. She sent him divorce papers during his second week in prison.

"You don't love him anymore?" I'd asked.

"It's not about loving him," she'd said. "It's about letting him go so I can have a life, too."

That was something I didn't know how to do.

It was visiting day at the Varner Unit of the Arkansas Department of Correction. The prison was about an hour and a half's drive from Creed and it usually had visiting day on the weekends. Unless Aunt Linda was working, she came every time. I couldn't come unless she did. They didn't let minors visit without an adult. Even so, I only came with her about once a month.

I wasn't claustrophobic, but every time I walked through the metal detectors, it felt like the walls were closing in. We made it through the line in record time. There weren't a lot of people visiting.

The visiting room was divided by a glass partition, with cubicles set up all along the glass. There was room for two visitors on one side and the inmate on the other, with a phone on either side of the partition.

There was a loud buzzing sound and the door opened and my dad walked into the room. I used to think he was the biggest man in the world, but every time I visited, he was smaller. I was taller than him now.

He sat in the chair across from us and picked up the phone. I picked up mine. Aunt Linda always let me go first. She'd bring a book or magazine, something to pay attention to, so that I could have some sort of privacy.

"Son," he said. He usually called me "son" instead of saying my name, like he was trying to remind me of my role.

"Dad," I said, returning the gesture.

I didn't know how thick the glass between us was. I used to wonder how much strength it'd take to break it. I'd imagine being able to do it. The times he was in county jail, they'd let us visit in an open room with tables and chairs. I could touch him. I didn't, but there was the option.

Looking at him was like looking in a mirror, only this mirror aged you twenty years. John looked more like my mom's side of the family, like Hank. I used to be jealous of that, because I thought that made it easier for John. He could pretend that he was Hank's son. I couldn't, because my dad was in the mirror every time I looked in one.

"Have you heard from John?" he asked.

It was always the first thing he asked.

"Not in a while," I said. "You?"

He shook his head. "You still with June?"

He thought he was asking another question he knew the answer to, like his first one. He didn't know that I'd betrayed her, that she was in the hospital and might never speak to me again.

"I don't know," I said. "It's complicated."

I didn't add that she might hate me now.

He leaned back in his seat. "It always is," he said.

He waited for me to explain, but I didn't trust myself to talk about it yet and there was really only one thing I'd come there to say.

"I got a letter from your mom," he said, interrupting my thoughts.

"Really?"

"Yeah, she married Larry."

He could tell this was news to me.

"I'm sure she was going to get around to telling you."

"Yeah," I said. She probably wanted my dad to know first.

"I guess Larry makes her happy," he said.

"I hope so."

He nodded.

"I'm quitting Benny's," I said. "I've got one more job to do and then I'm done with him."

He shifted in his seat, like he couldn't get comfortable, and then he leaned closer to the glass.

"You're gonna be an upstanding citizen now?" he asked. His look was a cross between proud and sad, like he knew this was the moment he'd lost me to Hank.

"I'm gonna try," I said.

"What will you do for cash?"

"I'm going to Hank's this summer," I said.

He nodded. "You always go to Hank's."

"I don't think I'm coming back."

His face changed. He leaned back in the seat, like he was chewing over the idea. Aunt Linda didn't look up from her book but she put her hand on my leg.

"I think that's a good idea," he said finally.

There was a twinge in my side, a tiny part of me that hurt, because I wanted him to ask me not to go. I wouldn't be able to see him once a month.

"You've got options I didn't have," he said. "If you've found your way out, then you should take it."

"And it's not like I have much in Creed to stick around for," I said.

It was a jab at him for not being around to raise me.

"It wasn't my choice to leave you, kid."

Not like my mom, he meant. I hated being put in the position of defending her, but I would do it and he knew it. And he was wrong. Somewhere along the way, he did make a choice.

He sat up straighter in his seat, like he was preparing for the fight.

I hung up the phone and stood, surprising both of us.

"Bye, Dad," I mouthed. "I'll see you."

CHAPTER 8

My birds were gone. A nurse had made me take a shower earlier and I couldn't find a trace of one. I'd been careful with them since being admitted, only showering when forced and then trying to save one or two. I'd wanted to keep the birds. I liked the idea of them wearing off over time.

Lifting the gown I'd been given over my head, I stood bare under the fluorescent lights of the bathroom and stared at my body in the mirror. I searched for the birds, just in case I had missed one.

Wait.

There on my left hip bone was a black smudge, a disappearing feather. I put my hand over it. It'd be my secret.

It felt good to have one.

My face was almost healed from the scratches. I didn't

know how I felt about that. The scratches were a clue that something was wrong inside my head. I imagined the "misfires" in my brain that Dr. Keels had talked about that made me see and hear things no one else could.

My eyes were sensitive to the light and my head felt fuzzy, both side effects of my medication. Dr. Keels had upped the dosage. She told me to expect the fuzzy-headed feeling for a while but she didn't say anything about the light. I had to remember to talk to her about it. I saw her every day and we talked endlessly about everything. She dissected my symptoms until they were cut into their smallest pieces. She'd been crossing possible causes of psychosis off her list.

~~Severe depression~~.

~~Bipolar disorder~~.

~~Lack of sleep~~.

I'd been getting regular sleep lately with the help of a sleeping pill, but my symptoms still persisted. I hadn't heard a voice since being admitted, but there were the other noises. At night, after everyone was asleep and the halls were dark, I'd hear someone walking down the hall. They always stopped outside my door. For a while they wouldn't knock, just stand out there breathing heavily. Then the knocking would begin. The first time it happened, I opened the door unaware, just like when I'd answer the door back home after hearing the doorbell. I thought maybe it was one of my parents coming to tell me good night. They were spending more time at the hospital than home lately. No one was there, and

I didn't take it well. Dr. Keels prescribed a stronger sleeping pill after that.

There was one cause of psychosis that Dr. Keels hadn't crossed off her list yet. We'd been dancing around the idea during our sessions, both the ones with just me and her and the ones with my parents.

Schizophrenia.

I was preparing myself for it to be that, reading everything I could, asking Dr. Keels a million questions. She told me not to get ahead of myself, that it had to be at least thirty days before a diagnosis was made. That was what she was leaning toward, though. I could tell. Unless my symptoms changed. My symptoms drove everything.

I asked her a million questions and she answered every one. She said that for some people, the onset of schizophrenia was like a slow burn, a gradual decrease in functioning over a period of time. For others, the onset could be sudden— something could happen to trigger the illness.

"Typically, the symptoms increase in frequency and severity until there is a break from reality," she said.

I'd had a break from reality.

"If this is schizophrenia, then it's a good sign that you're experiencing more positive symptoms than negative ones," she said.

"What's positive about my symptoms?"

"*Positive* means something different in this context. Hearing voices and seeing things are occurrences you've never experienced before. They're added characteristics, positives. Negative symptoms are the absence of your normal characteristics. Not sleeping is a negative symptom. Others would be lack of motivation, social withdrawal, inability to maintain relationships, problems with speech and movement. Negative symptoms impact quality of life more so than positive ones."

"So what do we do about it?" I asked.

"What we're doing now," she said.

"But you still don't know for sure."

"We can't know for sure yet," she said.

It amazed me how much guesswork went into making a diagnosis. I wanted it to be an exact science, but that wasn't the case. There was no blood test.

I'd been in the hospital fifteen days now. They were talking about transitioning me back home soon. I was equal parts excited and terrified. Part of me worried that I was making progress only because I was at the hospital, in a controlled environment, and as soon as I checked out, the voices would come back. Dr. Keels promised me that they wouldn't just send me out the door, though. She said we'd start with night visits and then weekend passes, gradually building up to spending weekdays at home, too. She said everything would go at a pace I was comfortable with.

There was a knock on the bathroom door and I put my gown back on. A nurse popped her head in. Her name was Rachel, and she looked young for her age, like the girls in my high school. I missed Janet, but she worked seven days on and seven days off. It was her week off. I knew Barry wasn't far behind Rachel. He never was. He was the orderly who was her shadow. He reminded me of a club bouncer. If people got out of control, Barry stepped in. I hadn't seen anything like that yet, but I didn't doubt that it happened. My bed came with restraints.

Rachel led me back to my room. It didn't have a window. None of the rooms they'd placed me in had windows. It made it impossible to know what time of day it was.

In addition to seeing Dr. Keels every day, I'd been sleeping and reading. I'd accrued a lot of sleep debt and I had to pay up. Dr. Keels called it recovery sleep. I'd read everything she'd given me. They didn't let me keep the materials at night, though. They took them away every evening and brought them back during the day. They probably worried I'd obsess over them like I had the college information. As if I could fight the sleeping pill.

They took my notebook away at night, too. I started a new section in it called "You're Not Crazy, You're Sick" and I wrote down the things I'd learned about schizophrenia that were the most important to me.

A person with schizophrenia could lead an independent, successful life.

A person with schizophrenia could experience recovery.

A person with schizophrenia could enjoy relationships,
have a job,
drive a car,

go to college,

love,

be loved.

A person with schizophrenia could experience all human emotions, because she was a real person. A person with schizophrenia could be happy.

I could be happy. Dr. Keels had said so and it said it on page eighteen of the *Living with Schizophrenia* pamphlet from the National Alliance of Mental Health and those guys couldn't be wrong.

There was a weird kind of relief in knowing that what I was experiencing could have a name and that there was a treatment plan. There were other people who felt like this, too. They heard things and saw things and they weren't crazy either, just sick, like me.

I was doing better, I had to be, because they were leaving me alone more and more. Nobody watched me pee anymore. That had to be a sign of improvement. I wouldn't admit it, but I was lonely. In the past couple of months, I hadn't had that much practice being alone. I'd started talking to myself.

What do you want to do today, June? I asked myself.

Oh, I don't know, I thought I'd sit on the bed for a while and then maybe go to the bathroom later.

That sounds like a fine plan for the day.

Sure, sure, and if I'm feeling up to it, I might just take a nap, or turn in circles in the middle of the room, who knows.

There was movement behind me and my face flushed

hot. I whipped around and Nick was there, standing in the doorway of my room, like magic. Just when I thought I was getting better. I'd never hallucinated him before, but maybe I was taking the wrong drug. He wore his usual uniform of scuffed-up jeans and white T-shirt. There were dots of blue paint on his hands. His face was somber and a little scared. Nick was hardly ever scared. Just when I was convinced he was never going to speak, he held up a piece of paper. It was a drawing of a window, and through it was a beautiful garden with flowers and a fountain. He pulled tape from his pocket and came into the room, shutting the door behind him. He taped the drawing on the wall across from my bed. When I lay on my side, I'd be able to see it.

I didn't know how he knew I was in a room with no window, but Nick always knew things about me he shouldn't. He came to sit on the bed with me. I wanted him to touch me, but he looked like he was scared I might break. I didn't think he was breathing. I still wasn't sure if he was real.

Tired of waiting, I reached out and covered a freckle on his face with my finger, right above his lip.

"I've never liked that freckle," I said.

He was warm and real. He smiled and my finger slipped from his face.

"How did you get in here?" I asked.

"I'm good at getting into places I shouldn't be," he said.

I'd missed him so much. I hadn't realized how much until this exact moment with him sitting half a foot from me, his eyes warm on my face, his mouth just like I remembered it.

"How did you get in here?" I asked again.

"My aunt Linda," he explained. He pulled her badge from underneath the collar of his shirt and touched the bar code at the bottom of it. "This can open any door."

"I haven't seen her since I've been here," I said.

"She's seen you, though. She's only here at night. She's kept me updated."

"You look tired," I said. The skin underneath his eyes looked bruised.

"I haven't slept so good since you've been here."

"You've been worried about me?"

"Yeah," he said, his voice low.

He reached out and took my hand and I closed my eyes, because it felt like coming home.

"Bethany said to give this to you." He pulled something from his pocket.

It was a letter, folded into fourths, with Bethany's pretty handwriting on the outside, *For June.*

"She wanted to come with me," he said. "But I knew it wouldn't be easy for me to get in here without getting noticed and two people would make it that much harder. She's currently not speaking to me."

"She'll forgive you," I said.

"Will you?" he asked. He looked like he had right after he'd found out John was being sent to Afghanistan. He looked like he was preparing to lose another person from his life. "I broke my promise to you," he said.

I tried to say something.

"I wanted to keep it, but I was scared. Me and Bethany weren't helping you by hiding it. I think we were hurting you. I think if it hadn't been for us, you would've asked your parents for help a long time ago, and I think you needed help a long time ago."

"It's okay."

His look said he didn't believe me.

"This was too important. You're too important," he said.

"It was the right thing to do," I said.

He looked like he was unsure that he could trust what I was saying.

"Tell me you forgive me," he said.

"I forgive you."

He didn't look convinced.

"Tell me everything will be all right," he said.

"I can't."

"Please?"

"I don't want to lie to you. Don't make me."

He thought about it and then nodded.

"I wanted to come sooner, but Aunt Linda said to give it some time, that you might need some time."

Those last words stumbled out of his mouth, like he'd tried to eat them back at the last minute.

"It wouldn't have done any good to come earlier," I said. "I've been pretty out of it. Today is one of the first days that I feel like I'm getting closer to being myself."

I'd almost forgotten what that felt like.

"What have you been doing?" he asked.

"Sleeping, mostly," I said.

"That's good."

"And I see Dr. Keels every day. She's the psychiatrist that's treating me."

I wanted to call her mine, as in *She's my psychiatrist,* but I didn't know how long Dr. Keels was sticking around Creed. That thought scared me, because I was already attached to her.

"What are they saying?" he asked. "What do they think it is?"

"I only have a working diagnosis right now."

Dr. Keels's words felt funny on my tongue. I was scared to tell him what it might be, scared he'd look at me differently.

"They're still trying to figure it out?"

I nodded.

"Well, they'll get it. It's their job."

The way he said *they* was like he believed there was a team of people working on it somewhere in the back. I imagined them in a room with one long table in the center of it. They'd sit around it, poring over papers and adjusting their glasses. There'd be a whiteboard with elaborate notes with pointing arrows and Venn diagrams.

I didn't want to disappoint him with the truth that at this hospital, it was just Dr. Keels and my dad. And me. Dr. Keels had told me I was the most important person in the equation.

I wanted to tell Nick what she thought it was. It would

be my first time saying the word out loud. My face felt hot. I didn't understand this feeling. I didn't understand why I felt ashamed.

"It could be schizophrenia," I said. I said it like a question.

My eyes stung and I waited for his gasp, or a look of revulsion, or a proclamation. *That can't be right. You're not crazy.*

He didn't say anything, though, just kept holding my hand, his eyes still looking like the sea.

"Hey," he said, reading the fear in my face. "It doesn't matter what it's called. I know who you are. Nothing can change that."

I wanted to believe him.

He looked around the room, assessing. I wondered what he thought of it.

"Would you like the tour?" I asked. "There's no need to stand. This is a sitting tour. Over there is a corner and about five feet to the left is another corner. Right here is a corner that looks exactly like the first two. This one over here is different—no, wait, I'm kidding, it's the same."

"You're such a smart-ass," he said, and smiled. "I'm glad that hasn't changed."

I wanted to talk about all the ways I hadn't changed, but he noticed the restraints on the sides of the bed and his face went hard. His aunt Linda probably hadn't told him about those.

"What the hell, June?" He picked one up and fingered the straps. His voice did that thing where the madder he got, the

– 140 –

quieter he got. "They're not using these on you, are they?" he whispered.

I shook my head. "They haven't had to so far."

"So far?" He looked like he wanted to burn the place down. "Does your dad know about this?"

I nodded. "It's okay. Everyone has been really great. They're super nice."

He looked like he didn't believe me.

"It was really scary at first, but I'm getting used to it. Dr. Keels said the restraints are there for the patients' safety, or for the staff's safety if it's someone who's violent."

I wasn't making him feel better. "I'm not violent, so I should be good," I said, smiling.

"Nothing about this is funny, June," he said.

"I know. This is the most unfunny thing that's ever happened to me."

"I'm sorry," he said.

I picked at the blue paint on his hand. "Have you been to the barn?"

"Yeah," he said guiltily. It was like he was worried I didn't want him going without me.

"It's okay," I said. "I've been imagining you there. It's helped."

Some of the paint from his hand was under my fingernails and I wondered how long I could keep it.

"If my parents ever let me out of their sight again, am I still invited to go with you when you go to Hank's?" I asked.

"Yeah," he said, with no hesitation. "I don't want to go without you."

"That's good, because I could use something to look forward to. When you see Bethany, tell her I love her and I miss her and thank her for the letter."

It didn't matter what it said, I was thankful for it. I felt like I was going to cry.

"Okay," he said.

"How did it feel to quit Benny's?" I asked, trying to divert the tears.

"Like someone cut a rope from around my neck."

"I'm proud of you."

He pulled back, letting go of my hand. "Don't be proud of me yet," he said.

"Why not?"

"I haven't seen you in days," he said. "I don't want to talk about Benny. Let's get out of here."

Another escape.

"I can't. I have to stay until they tell me it's okay to go home."

"I don't mean out of here out of here, just out of this room. Let's go to the roof. I want to show you something."

As much time as I'd spent in the hospital with my parents, I'd never gone to the roof. It had never occurred to me.

"Why? Is there this thing you want to do to me?" I asked, repeating his words from the other day at school.

"Well, yeah," he said, smiling. "But I didn't bring paint."

My smile fell, remembering the birds.

"What?" he asked.

"I only have one feather left," I said, putting my hand over the last feather where it sat under my gown, right by my hip.

His eyes went to my hand. "It's okay," he said. "I'll paint them back. I promise. Now come on. Let's go. How close do they watch you?"

"Close. I'm a mental patient."

He smirked. "I'll have you back before anyone notices."

Saying no to him was something I'd never been good at. I stood, putting on the cotton booties they'd given me. It was either those or flip-flops. No shoelaces allowed on this floor.

"I might be clumsy," I said. "I'm still getting used to the meds." I winced when I looked up. "And the lights."

"I'll help you," he said, his hand grabbing on to mine. "I won't let you fall. It'll be worth it, I promise."

Walking to the door, he said, "Don't look like you're sneaking. The trick is acting like you know what you're doing. Walk with purpose. Everyone will think you have permission to do whatever it is you're doing."

He stuck his head out the door. "Let's go."

We moved down the hall as stealthily as a boy and a mental patient getting used to antipsychotic medication could move. When we came around the corner, we saw Nurse Rachel and Barry. We ducked down a hall and hid in a janitor's closet. The smell of cleaner was sharp and my eyes watered. His face was close to mine, our breathing loud in the small space. He smiled and I didn't want to do anything else but stare at his face. I was excited. All this time I'd spent in the hospital, I'd felt like I was moving underwater, and just a few minutes with Nick and everything was real again.

When we thought it was safe, we ventured out and made it to the stairwell. The stairs proved difficult. I imagined what a heart patient felt like after surgery, my hand going to my chest to keep my heart from beating out of my body. I didn't know if this was a side effect of the drug or of me lying still for days.

He pushed open the door to the roof and a part of me was surprised that there was no alarm. He tried to pull me along, but the sun stopped me. I kept my eyes down, thinking they'd adjust. So far the sensitivity to light was the hardest side effect to deal with. Nick pulled his backpack off and reached inside it. He pulled sunglasses out and put them on my face.

"Is that better?" he whispered, his voice soft and so close.

"Yeah."

"I want to show you this. It's special." He led me to the far corner. "My aunt Linda told me about it."

I followed him. He squatted down in front of the half wall that went around the perimeter of the building. There were names, so many of them, carved into the concrete.

Mary was here.

Cody was here.

Brittany was here.

Kendrick was here.

Logan, Faith, Emily, Broderick, Amber, Jake.

They were all here.

Dawn, Melissa, Courtney, Kate, Erin, Susan, Mike, Kurt, Ronald, Eliza.

They were here, too. I thought of John carving his name into things before he left Creed.

Nick read my mind and pointed to a spot, his finger running over the name.

John was here.

"Your John?" I asked.

He nodded.

"When did he do that?"

Nick shrugged. "Aunt Linda thinks it was one day when she asked him to come pick her up from work. She wasn't ready to leave and he went exploring."

"Who are they?" I asked.

"Aunt Linda says they're patients, mostly. She's seen some of them sneak up here at night."

I imagined the patients sneaking out of their rooms and onto the roof so they could add their names to the wall, so they could be part of something, or to leave proof that they were here. I wondered how many of them were from the fourth floor.

He reached in his backpack and pulled out a pocketknife and opened it. "Let's add ours," he said.

I nodded. I couldn't explain the need to be a part of it, but it was there.

I squatted down next to him. I felt dizzy. "I don't think I should hold a knife right now."

"I'll do it," he said.

He pressed his knife to the concrete under John's name and started carving, concrete dust falling to the roof floor. When he was done, he stood. He took my hand and we backed up so we could see it better.

Nick and June were here.

Unless something happened to this building, there'd always be evidence that we were here, together. It felt important.

We slipped back into my room and Nick checked the time on his phone.

"I have to go," he said. "Aunt Linda said they serve dinner at five."

"Yeah, it's the early bird special every day."

I got in the bed and under the covers. I was exhausted from our field trip.

"So I guess I'll go," he said.

But instead of walking out the door, he sat on the bed next to me and reached for my hand.

"Yeah," I said. "You should go." But I squeezed his hand tighter, pulling him closer. "Try to get some sleep tonight."

His eyes were on the restraints again.

"I'll be fine. I promise."

He scooted closer to me, the covers bunching between us, his knee touching my hip, right above the feather, but he still wasn't looking at me. I wanted to distract him from the restraints.

"There was a girl and a boy," I said.

He lifted his eyes and looked at me.

"The girl was sick," I said.

He pulled me even closer to him. "And the boy was bad," he added.

"Not as bad as he thought, though."

He ran his fingers across my forearm and it took me a minute to realize he was drawing a bird, his fingers tracing along the feathers.

"The girl didn't know what to do next," I whispered.

"The boy never knew what to do."

"She was scared."

He rested his forehead against mine. "So was he. Maybe they could figure it out together," he said.

"Maybe," I said.

"Was there a dragon?" he asked. There was a hopeful sound in his voice.

"There was a dragon."

CHAPTER 9

It was the first summer I'd spent at Hank's since my dad had gone to prison, and the sound of wood splintering was my new favorite sound. The hammer became an extension of me. There was a moment when I brought the hammer down on the furniture and found the weak spot in the wood and I knew it would only take a couple more hits before it would break. I was in the workshop behind the cabin. I'd busted up four chairs already. They were ones I'd built, so I figured they were mine to break.

"What are you doing?" John asked.

He came in from the back door and dropped a pile of wood at his feet. He walked toward me, but I thrust my arm out so he'd see that he needed to stop where he was. There was a hole at my feet, and if he got too close, he'd fall in. We'd both be stuck in this pit. Uncle Hank walked in right after him and took in the scene around him, me pointing the hammer at John, the splintered heaps of broken furniture all around me. He came right for me, like he couldn't see the hole I was standing in, or if he could, he didn't care. He jerked the hammer away from me and tossed it to the side.

"Get out of here," he said to John. He didn't take his eyes off me.

Once we were alone, he kicked at the broken chairs at our feet. "Is there a reason you're undoing all of your hard work?"

"They weren't good chairs anyway," I said. "I don't know what I'm doing."

"Sure you do." He bent down and started picking up the wood. "Help me," he said.

I didn't move. He stood.

"Help me," he repeated.

He thrust his gathered pieces of wood into my hands. "We'll get this cleaned up and then you'll go out back and help John cut the rest of the wood."

"What's the point?" I asked.

"The point is I need the wood cut. You can't make furniture without cutting the wood first."

"Then what?" I asked.

He knew I wasn't just asking him what to do after the wood was cut.

"You don't have to have it all figured out right now," he said.

My nose burned. I was going to cry and I didn't even know why. I had so much anger in me. There was so much that was out of my control.

It was my hardest summer at the cabin, but by the end of it, I was feeling better. The Ozarks held a special kind of quiet, the kind of quiet I wanted to take with me back to Creed.

"There's no place like this at home," I told Uncle Hank.

We'd been outside, stretching canvas all day. We always spent our last day of the summer doing this, so he'd have plenty to paint on during the year.

"What do you mean?" he asked.

"Someplace where I can just be and not worry about everything."

I'd made a lot of progress over the summer and I wanted to hold on to it.

"I know of a place," he said. "It's kind of a secret."

"In Creed?"

"Do you know where the Franklin farm is?"

I nodded. The Franklins had been one of the founding families of the town, but they'd left a long time ago. They'd never sold their property. The farm was a hundred acres of grown-up grass and not much else.

"There's a barn at the back of the property, near the woods. You can't see it from the road. It was a place I used to go to when I needed things to get quiet. I made it my own, brought some of my stuff there. I didn't really have a place that was just mine at home. The barn became that place. You could go there. It's probably ready to fall down, though, so you'll have to be careful. You'll need to replace a lot of the boards in the loft if you want to use it. But that won't be a problem for you now."

It wouldn't be.

"And it'd keep your hands busy."

I needed that. "You won't mind?"

"I wouldn't be telling you about it if I did."

He seemed tense, though, like he might've regretted it.

"It started out as just a place," he said. "Then it became something more."

The sun poured into the space through the loft window of the barn. I was lying on the cot, face to face with one of Hank's paintings. It was of the high school and the railroad tracks behind it.

I didn't know what time it was, but it was late in the day, by the looks of it. I'd spent most nights here since June had been admitted to the hospital. I'd paint until I couldn't see anymore and then crash on the cot in the loft. I'd been up late the night before. I'd tried to rest like June had wanted, but I couldn't stop thinking about her sleeping in a bed that came with straps to tie her down. And then once I'd fallen asleep, I'd had a nightmare.

I'd known I was dreaming, because we were in the barn

and June was dancing. June never danced. She moved to music I couldn't hear. She was free in a way I'd never seen her in real life, her movements unmeasured. I didn't want to look away from her, but John was there, too. I hadn't dreamed about him in a long time. There was a TV in the loft, and an Xbox. John sat in front of it and held out a controller. There wasn't electricity in the barn, but it didn't matter in this dream.

"Wanna play?" he asked.

"Yeah," I said, taking the controller from him.

There was something different about him, but I couldn't put my finger on it. He wore the desert camo I'd seen in one of the pictures he'd sent me from Afghanistan. The camo was worn now, though, and ripped in places. He looked like he'd been left outside for too long, his face tan from spending so much time in the desert.

We played for a while, June dancing around us. Then it hit me, why he looked different.

He was dead.

That was what was wrong with his eyes. I saw the wound then, a hole in his side, and the stains on his camo where the blood had dried.

I'd woken up with a start and now John was in my head and I couldn't get him out of it. For a second I'd forgotten he wasn't somewhere where he could take calls and I'd picked up my phone to call him. I really needed to talk to him. I needed to know that he was okay and for him to tell me what to do next. I couldn't call June either and Hank didn't have a phone, so there was nobody to talk to, nobody to tell me that it was just a dream, nothing to do but stare at Hank's painting.

I dialed John's number anyway. When his voice mail picked up, my stomach hit my feet.

"It's John. Don't leave a voice mail, because nobody checks those."

The beep sounded.

"Hey, man, it's Nick. I know you won't get this. I just wanted to talk to you. I hope you're okay. I haven't heard from you in a while. I hope you've been getting the drawings I've sent you. I'm bringing June with me to Hank's this summer. We can take her out there, to our spot. She'll love it. She's looking forward to coming. She's not been doing so good lately. Anyway, I hope I hear from you soon."

I hung up. My phone rang a second later and I answered it so fast, like there was a chance that it was John calling me back.

"Hello?"

"The car I was telling you about will be in the area tonight," Benny said.

He was the last person I wanted to talk to. I hadn't heard from him in days. Part of me had wondered if he'd forgotten that he'd offered me double to steal a car. Part of me hoped that he had.

"Come to the garage and I'll give you the details." He hung up without waiting for me to say anything.

I didn't want to go to the garage. I couldn't shake my

dream. I wanted to see June again, but it'd be stupid to push my luck and I couldn't risk Aunt Linda's job any more than I already had. So I did the one thing I didn't want to do and went to the garage.

I'd been there for an hour. Benny had told me to wait outside. I wished I hadn't told him I'd do it. I wanted to be free already. Especially after seeing the look on June's face when she'd said she was proud of me. That was the thing, though. Once you agreed to a job, you had to go through with it or pay one of the other guys to do it. It was the way Benny kept us from agreeing to shit we couldn't really do just because he dangled some extra money in front of us. Nobody reneged on Benny. Only a couple of guys ever had, and they'd showed back up at the garage busted up so bad that they had a hard time walking.

I checked my phone. Correction: I'd been there an hour and fifteen minutes. Benny's favorite game was telling guys to come to the garage and then acting like he didn't know why we were there. We were his puppets. I kept my hands in my pockets so I didn't start punching things: my car, the brick wall behind me, Tommy, who wouldn't stop looking at me.

"What?" I asked him.

"I can't believe you're quitting."

"Believe it," I said. "I'm getting out of here."

"It's gonna suck without you here."

"It sucks now," I said, trying to take the anger out of my voice.

"Yeah, but when you're gone it'll be worse."

"You could quit, too."

"And do what?" he asked.

The side door to the garage opened and Benny stuck his head out. "Get in here," he said to me.

Following him inside, I thought about this being my last time in the garage. Some of my best memories were here. I knew that was screwed up.

We stepped into his office.

"Close the door," Benny said.

He sat at his desk and opened an envelope.

"It's a '97 Crown Vic," he said. "Black." He slid a picture of the car across the desk. "It'll be in El Dorado tonight at the downtown theater. It should be there by eight o'clock."

I picked up the photo. "Should Tommy go with me?" I asked.

"No, he's got shit to do here. Somebody'll bring you back to your car later."

I waited to see if there were more instructions, but he just stared at me.

"I meant what I said the other day," I said.

He gave me a confused look.

"On the phone. When I said this was the last one. I meant it."

He studied my face for a long time. I didn't know what

he saw there. The only sounds came from outside the office, tools clanging, pumps breathing. He kept staring.

Finally he grunted. "A lot of guys have sat just where you're sitting and said the same thing. They always come back, though." He leaned forward. "You need me more than you think you do."

"I don't. I don't need you."

"We'll see about that," he said.

I didn't care if he believed me. I wouldn't disappoint June. I'd wanted to come clean in the hospital and tell her that I had one more job to do, but I knew it would have upset her. I was the last thing she needed to worry about.

"Get going," he said. "I'll expect you back here by ten." His look said he knew this wasn't going to be my last job.

It had been dark for a while and I'd been driving around El Dorado, wasting time. I'd had to get out of Creed earlier. I'd kept driving by the hospital, like I was making sure it was still there.

Parking on a side street across from the theater, I spotted the car. Under any other circumstances, I'd never pick this car to steal, not where it was. The theater was in the middle of downtown and there were too many other businesses around, too many windows looking out on the street. I thought about waiting for whoever owned it to come back and following them to wherever they went next. Maybe it'd be a more secluded spot. But Benny wanted me and the car back in a couple of hours.

Reaching under my seat, I grabbed my tools. This was the last time. As stupid as it was, part of me was sad to let go of something that my dad had taught me how to do. We didn't share a lot.

What was even more screwed up was that part of me still missed the days when we had done it together, me being his lookout during those years when I was too young to steal a car by myself. I'd been his lookout more times than I could count, my back pressed against the car while he worked the lock. The first time I'd helped him, he had the door open and me in the car in no time. The feeling was amazing, my dad's laugh loud when he saw I was excited. It was a "That's my boy" moment. I knew that stealing was wrong, that what we were doing was wrong, but I was his boy.

It was time to let it go, though. I could do it. I could make a break from this life. I opened my car door and stepped into the street. I could be who June wanted me to be.

The street was lined with cars, but nobody was around. Probably everyone was inside the theater. I didn't know who the car belonged to, or when they'd be back for it, and my heartbeat picked up. I didn't know what was inside it, or why Benny wanted it, but I knew I needed to stop thinking about the things I didn't know.

I walked up to the car and slid the lock pick between the window and the door. "One fluid motion," my dad would say. The lock made the click noise that let me know I was in. What if I was never as good at something else as I was at this? I opened the car door and dropped down into the seat. I had it cranked in no time.

There was movement in my periphery. It was one of those moments that I'd rewind in my mind over and over again, trying to find the exact moment when it had all gone to shit, trying to figure out what I'd missed.

The car door was still open and I noticed the smell of a man's aftershave. The hairs stood on the back of my neck and I gripped the tool still in my hand.

"Stop what you're doing and step out of the car," he said. His voice was older, gruff.

Time stopped moving. I opened my mouth to try and get a good breath, because the air stopped moving, too. I got out of the car. I couldn't see him. He was behind me.

"Put your hands in the air. Slowly."

I almost couldn't hear him over my heartbeat hammering in my ears. I was hot in an instant, sweat dripping off my forehead. *What would John do?* I thought. A flashlight shone on the back of my head now. John would run. He'd never been arrested. He was almost shot once, but he'd never been arrested. I could run, too. I could knock back into him, throw him off balance, and run like hell. I was fast.

"Drop your tools," he said.

The metal made a quiet clanking sound against the street. *Run.*

"Turn around. Keep your hands up," he said.

I was going to run.

I turned. I couldn't see his face because of the flashlight now shining in my eyes, but I saw his uniform, his utility belt, his badge, the gun pointing at my face. It wasn't the first time one had been pointed at me, but never this close before. There was no way I could run without getting shot.

The air left my body in one slow exhale until there was no more breath in me.

He reached for me, pulling cuffs from his side. They were on me in a second, cold and pinching, and he turned me to face the car, pushing my face to the hood. It was still warm. I didn't resist and he didn't have to tell me what to do next. This was a dance I knew.

It was over. There was a feeling, a sick kind of relief. I could stop dreading it now, because this was always going to happen. This wasn't gonna go like the last two times I was arrested. The judge had warned me the last time that I wouldn't see the inside of a juvenile courtroom again. I was going to real jail. Maybe they'd put me near my dad. I wondered if he'd be surprised to see me, or worse, if I'd get a "That's my boy" smile.

This shouldn't hurt, because this was where I'd always been headed. Why did it hurt?

"That your car back there?" he asked.

He hefted me up and turned me to face the way I'd come. He must've been watching me.

"Or did you steal that one, too?"

I didn't say anything and he pushed me to my knees, the tiny rocks on the pavement pushing back into them.

"Don't move," he said.

The news of this would reach Creed before I did. June would get out of the hospital soon. She'd find out. She'd know she was wrong about me. I couldn't be who she wanted. My face burned and it felt like I'd been kicked in the stomach. I opened my mouth, trying to take in more breath. I'd wanted the chance to be the guy she thought I was.

CHAPTER 10

When we were in the fifth grade, we went on a field trip to the zoo and June got separated from the group. Somehow we'd lost her after the otter exhibit. The parents and teachers took kids and split up, trying to find her. I snuck away from my group, because they were moving too slow and I had an idea of where she might've gone. I'd noticed that she hadn't wanted to leave the monkey cages when everybody else did. I found her sitting on a bench in front of the cages, staring at one of the monkeys. The monkey was so still, looking back at her. I'd never seen one sit so still. June looked sad, like she was about to cry.

I sat next to her on the bench. "What's wrong?" I asked.

She didn't look at me, just kept staring at the monkey.

"I think he knows," she said.

"Knows what?"

"That he's never going anywhere."

I felt sad, too, even though I didn't really understand why. I scooted closer to her on the bench. All I really knew was that I wanted to get closer to her.

It was the same way even now. There was so much I didn't understand, but being closer to June made it easier. I thought about that day at the zoo a lot, wondering if that was why June was drawn to me, why she sometimes looked sad when she looked at me. Maybe I was like the monkey.

The bunk beds were crammed into a room too small for thirty-six boys to sleep in, but Durrant Juvenile Correctional Center made it work. The snores, the coughs, every time someone rolled over—everything made it impossible to sleep. Even if I could block out all of the noise, my mattress was so thin that the springs pushed into my back, so even with my eyes closed, I couldn't forget where I was.

I'd been there a few days. Because I was a minor, they had to keep me there until the trial. There was nothing else to do but replay that night in my head and count all the ways I'd screwed up my life. The memories ran on a loop, right next to the image of June's face in the hospital when she'd said she was proud of me. What hurt the most was that I wouldn't be able to take her to Hank's this summer.

My court-appointed lawyer had come to visit me the day

before. He looked my age. I could tell juvie made him nervous. I almost asked him if this was his first case.

"You're going to be tried as an adult," he said.

He acted like he'd delivered unexpected news.

"Based on your priors and the possession of the gun, you're being charged with a Class B felony."

They'd searched my car and found the gun I kept in the glove compartment. Benny made us each keep one in case it was needed for intimidation purposes, but I never took it out.

"You're looking at a minimum of five years. The maximum penalty is fifteen."

"I thought my priors couldn't be used against me." That was one perk of committing crimes when you were a kid.

"In Arkansas, if the crimes are similar, prosecutors can push to have them included if they want to enhance the charge in the adult case. It establishes a pattern of behavior." He opened the file he'd brought with him.

"But they won't give me fifteen years," I said.

His look said I was wrong.

"For *trying* to steal a car?"

"You work at Benny's Garage?" he asked.

"Yeah."

"For how long?"

"Almost four years."

"And you've been arrested three times now, counting this time, all for the same crime."

"You have my file right in front of you. You know everything."

His look said he knew he didn't. "The prosecutor is trying to make an example of you. Everyone in Creed knows who Benny Robertson is, what he does."

I kept my face still. Everyone knew who Benny was, and nobody had ever cared before.

"Are you aware that in the last five years, four other employees have been arrested and convicted of grand theft auto?"

"Yes."

"And one of them was your father, correct?"

"I'm aware."

He lowered his voice. "If something bigger is going on here, then you need to tell me. For your sake."

Something bigger was going on. I was the fall guy. I wasn't getting out of there, and if I wanted even the minimum sentence, I'd have to rat on Benny. I thought about Tommy and all of the other boys who worked for Benny. Ratting out Benny would be ratting them out, too.

The lawyer looked frustrated. "Benny has a lot of underage boys working at the garage."

"Was that a question?" My temper rose. I knew it wasn't this guy's fault that my life had burned around me, but he was the one in front of me.

"No," he said. "Are you being coerced into stealing cars for your employer?"

"No."

"Are you being paid to steal cars for your employer?"

"No."

"To your knowledge, does the garage sell stolen car parts?"

"No," I bit out.

"Do you realize you'll be thirty-two when you get out of prison as a convicted felon?"

His words punched me in the stomach.

Fifteen years. I was seventeen. By the time I got out of jail, I'd have spent almost half my life there. I wondered who I'd be then.

"Yes," I said.

"And you don't have a problem with that? Because I would." He leaned close to me, like he was going to tell me a secret. "I wouldn't give years of my life for a man who wouldn't do the same for me. Benny Robertson has never been arrested. Isn't it time the right person gets punished?"

"No one made me do it," I said. "I broke into the car. It was my gun."

He stared at me in disbelief. "The prosecutor offered protection for the other guys working there, on any information you supply on old cases," he said. "He only wants Benny. Now, anything they do after today is on them."

"So if I tell you what you want to hear, they'll let me out of here?"

"If you take the deal, you'll be guaranteed the minimum sentence," he said.

"I'll still get five years?"

"With good behavior, you could be out sooner, but you're not walking away from this without jail time, not with your other offenses and the possession of the firearm. The judge would never go for it."

Five years or fifteen. That was what it came down to. I thought about June, what she would do when she found out. I felt sick to my stomach. I was the monkey in the cage and I wasn't going anywhere.

It was visiting day and Aunt Linda was on the list. I was equal parts excited and scared. I wondered if that was how my dad felt when we came to see him. I really wanted to see her, because I missed her, but I didn't want to see her disappointment or the look of resignation that was bound to be on her face. She'd predicted this. I'd almost told her not to come, but I was dying to know how June was doing and if she was home from the hospital. I'd gotten phone privileges the day before, but I'd been too chickenshit to call June. I was worried that she didn't have her phone and I didn't want to risk talking to her parents. Every time I talked to them, her dad especially, I was scared I'd hear the regret in their voices, like they were sorry they ever let me get close.

On visiting day, they put us in the cafeteria, one boy to a table. The other seats were for family members. There were always a lot of wasted seats at my table. Aunt Linda came in the room and I stood. At the first sight of her face, I knew something was very wrong, more than just the fact that I'd been arrested again. She looked stricken.

She got to my table.

"Dad?" I asked.

I hated the hopeful sound in my voice, but if something had happened to someone, I needed it to be him and not John.

She shook her head. "Billy is fine," she said, her voice tired.

"Who, then?"

It wasn't June, because June was safe. She was at the hospital or she was home. It was John. It hadn't been just a dream that I'd had the other night. Aunt Linda was coming to tell me that John was dead. He'd been killed in Afghanistan.

At first she didn't say anything, only put her arms around me, and I let her, for just a second.

"I'm so sorry," she said.

John was gone. That was why I hadn't heard from him. A dead guy couldn't write emails or make phone calls.

"Who is it?" I asked.

"A package came in the mail yesterday."

A package. A package had made her face look like that.

"Your mom called me a few days ago, the day after you got arrested."

My mom almost never called, and when she did, she didn't talk to Aunt Linda. She always said she could feel Aunt Linda's judgment through the phone.

"She was so upset. It was hard to understand her. She said to expect a package."

"What was in it?"

"Your uncle Hank had a heart attack."

I pressed my hands flat on the table and realized that I was no longer standing. It felt like someone had let all the air out of the room and then lit a match inside my gut.

"Your mama was so upset," she said. "It was hard to understand her. Even though they didn't see each other much, those two were close."

Nothing made sense. Aunt Linda felt bad for my mom. That was how fucked up things were.

He'd had a heart attack. They *were* close. Hank understood my mom in a way no one else did. He'd tried to help me understand her, too. He was the only reason I didn't hate her.

"How bad is it?" I asked.

But didn't I know the answer to that?

"He died, baby," she said, confirming my suspicion.

She covered my hands with hers where they still pressed against the table.

"He'd been setting fence posts," she said. "It was John who found him."

I couldn't speak, could barely breathe. It felt like cold water being thrown on me and suddenly the fire was out. It was a mistake.

"John's not home. There's a mistake."

Hank wasn't dead and John wasn't home.

"John is in Afghanistan," I said. My voice was calm and it surprised me. Maybe it was because I knew this was impossible. "I don't know why my mom is doing this, why she called you, but she lied to you. I don't know why. She likes drama, but John isn't home, so Hank can't be dead."

"I know this is hard to take in," she said. "I don't know why John was there. Your mom just said he was back. He found Hank right after it happened. She said John did everything he could to try and save him. He gave him CPR and then he hauled him in Hank's truck and got him to the hospital all by himself."

The nearest hospital was an hour away.

"He did all he could do," Aunt Linda said again. She shook her head over and over. "John didn't take it good. At all. Your mom said they had to call the police to the hospital when it was time to take the body away. Said they had to pull John off of Hank."

"Why didn't you tell me before now? I've been here for days."

"This was the first day they'd let me come out here. I wasn't telling you something like this over the phone." She had tears in her eyes. "Your mama tried calling you the day it happened, over and over, she said, but she couldn't get you."

She couldn't get me, because I was getting arrested.

"There isn't money for a coffin or a funeral," Aunt Linda said. "And your mama didn't know what else to do." Aunt

Linda looked ashamed, like this was her fault. "The county morgue gave her a good deal to cremate him."

The truth hit me in the gut. The package was Uncle Hank. The fire was back again.

"She mailed his ashes?" I asked. My voice rose an octave and I cleared it. "She mailed him to Creed?" I asked again. I was repeating myself, but I had trouble wrapping my mind around what she was saying.

"She thought he should come home. He came today. Priority Mail."

But the Ozarks were his home. They sent his ashes by Priority Mail. How did everything fall apart in such a short time?

"Your mom didn't see the point in waiting. She said she wanted it taken care of."

My mom didn't like leaving things undone. Once her mind was made up to do something, you couldn't change it.

Uncle Hank had never wanted to leave the mountain, though. Ever. The first summer I'd stayed with him, he'd showed me and John the place on the hill, the one in the painting that hung on Aunt Linda's wall in her kitchen. It was the place he'd stood when he knew he'd made the right decision to leave Creed.

"This is it," he'd said.

"What?" I'd asked.

"From this spot, I can see the cabin and the forests and everything behind it. The first time I stood here, I knew this place was where I was meant to be. This is the spot," he'd said.

Now he was a package. The man who'd showed me a different way was dust in a box in my aunt Linda's kitchen. My mom had mailed him to Creed. She had to have known that he wouldn't have wanted that, that he had never wanted to come back. But maybe she didn't.

"I thought I'd buy an urn, a pretty one," Aunt Linda said. "We could put him on the mantel. Isn't that where you're supposed to put a person's ashes?" she asked.

I couldn't answer.

"Maybe when you get out we can have a ceremony or something," she said. "We can borrow one of the preachers in town."

She didn't know it was going to be at least five years. I'd planned on breaking the news to her today.

"Mayb—"

"Stop," I said.

I needed her to stop talking. The fire in my stomach was spreading quickly, moving up my throat. She waited for me to say something else but I was afraid to open my mouth.

"I'm so sorry, Nick," she said finally. "I know what he meant to you."

"Where's John now?"

She shrugged. "Your mama thinks he went back to Hank's, but she's not sure. He left the hospital before the cremation."

"Is June still in the hospital?" I asked.

Aunt Linda looked confused by the change in conversation but then said, "She's been spending nights at home. I think they're getting ready to release her soon."

June knew where I was, then.

"There's some money in a box under my bed," I said.

"Nick, I do—"

"I know you were planning on getting a roommate, but that was down the road, and the rent is due in a couple of days."

"It's okay," she said.

"It's not okay," I said. "Nothing is okay anymore, but let me take care of this one thing. It's not a lot, less than five hundred, but it'll help you get by for now."

"You're always taking care of everyone else."

"You take care of me, too," I said.

I wanted to thank her for always doing right by me, for taking me in when I didn't have anywhere else to go, but I was worried if I did, I'd tip her off that I was saying goodbye, so I just said, "Thank you."

"For what?"

"For all of it."

"You're welcome, baby."

The guard across the room gave the signal. Time was up.

We hugged and I tried to memorize everything about her, how soft she was and how even though her perfume was cheap, it smelled sweet on her skin. She walked out of the room and I didn't look away, even though I wanted to, even though it would've been easier to.

Five years or fifteen. Uncle Hank was dead and John was home and nobody had told me. Nobody had called or said shit to me. Uncle Hank was dead. John had been with him. Five years or fifteen.

Nothing made sense. I looked out the window to make sure the sky was still blue.

I went back into the rec hall and got in line to use one of the phones. We could use them during our free time, but we only got ten minutes. I wanted to call John and ask him what had happened, demand to know why he was back early and why no one had thought I'd want to know.

I was pissed. The anger surged through me, and I was grateful for it. Anger was easier to handle in here. I'd have to be sad later. I was mad at John for coming home months early and not thinking I'd want to know, mad at him for being the one with Hank at the end. Mad at my mom for sending Hank's ashes home. Hank had never wanted to leave the mountain. Never.

I picked up the phone.

Five years or fifteen.

I thought about calling my lawyer and telling him my mind was made up, but I figured he could find out when everybody else did.

Instead I called the one person I knew who would help me do something this stupid. He answered on the second ring and accepted the charges.

"Shit, man. Do you know what this call is going to cost me?" Tommy asked.

"I'm good for it," I lied.

"How is everything?" he asked.

Tommy had a tone to his voice that only boys who'd been to juvie before had. He'd asked about ten questions with that one.

How's the food this time?

Is anybody messing with you?

Do you remember how to fight?

Is Justin still there? Is he still a dick?

Did they put the doors back on the bathroom stalls?

"It's the same," I said, answering all of them. "I need you to do something for me."

"Whatever you need."

It was exactly the answer I wanted.

"I need you to pick up some things for me and take them to that place I told you about."

There was silence for a moment. "All right," he said. "What do you need?"

"Go to my aunt Linda's house, but it has to be when she's not there. She'll be out tomorrow night after six."

She played cards every Wednesday night with Mrs. Walton, the lady who lived down the street. It was her only night off.

"There's a hide-a-key under the flowerpot by the front door."

"Okay . . . ," he said.

"Go to my room and get my backpack. I think I left it on my desk."

I kept a couple of changes of clothes in it at all times. I never knew when I'd need them.

"And then I need you to look on the kitchen counter by the refrigerator. That's where she keeps the mail. There should be a Priority Mail box. Put it in my backpack and bring it with you."

"Whatever you're thinking is probably a bad idea," Tommy said.

I didn't answer.

"All right, man. I'll do it," he said.

"Thanks, Tommy. I'll make it up to you."

I didn't know how. I hung up.

I'd leave the next day. The food truck came on Wednesdays. I'd slip out of the rec hall and hide in the back of the truck. I'd have to figure out how to get around the guards. I knew two of them were in the kitchen at all times. They might be easy enough to slip by, but I didn't know if there were any more guards once I was outside—other than the one by the fence, at the exit gate, but I'd be hiding in the back of the truck by the time I got to him. Maybe I could do it. It was how this kid Colton had broken out the last time I was here. Hopefully security hadn't been tightened up since then. I could do this. Boys broke out all the time. They were always caught, though, including Colton, because the only place they had to run to was home.

But I wasn't running home. The choice wasn't five years or fifteen. Not anymore. I'd get my bag from Tommy and then I'd make things right with Uncle Hank. If I couldn't take back how I'd left things with him, what I'd said, I could at least take his ashes back to his cabin. Hopefully John would be there and he'd explain to me what the hell he was doing home and we'd bury Hank on that spot on the hill.

Then I was going to do what I'd wanted to do for a long time, what I'd been hoping to do with Hank's blessing. I was going up the mountain. I'd disappear like Hank had and go off-grid. Hank had told me all about the people who had helped him. But first I had to see June. I had to make her believe that this was the only choice for me. She had to understand. Then I had to convince her to come with me.

CHAPTER 11

A couple of years ago, we went on a church trip. My parents had the same trouble picking a religion that they had deciding what type of dog would work best for our family, so we'd tried a few different ones. That summer, we were Methodists. I hadn't been excited to go, but then my parents agreed to let Bethany and Nick come, too. It was after Nick's first arrest and he'd just gotten out of Durrant. My dad thought it'd be good for him. We stayed at this place in the mountains called Church Campground, which we found out was a recently renovated chicken farm. The dorms were the old chicken coops. Even though it'd been a while since chickens had been kept there, you'd still see a floating feather from time to time. There was a girls' side and a boys' side, even for adults, so it was me and Bethany with my mom and Nick with my dad. It was the first time Nick and my dad spent a lot of time together just the two of them.

So much went wrong on that trip. Our first day, they'd scheduled a bonding exercise and we went canoeing on this lake a couple of miles away. It was fine at first, but we all missed the pickup point and had to walk back, pulling canoes upstream. We'd all left our shoes on the bank, and when we returned to the bank, they were gone. Someone had stolen fifty-two pairs of shoes from church campers. When we got back to the campground, the owners announced there would be an ice-cream and pool party, to cheer everyone up from the canoe disaster. The pool was only five feet deep, so you couldn't use the diving board, and all they served was ice-cream sandwiches. The whole thing felt like a challenge. The Methodists said it was a test of our faith. Theresa Reynolds snapped a picture of us about two seconds after my dad had gone into a hysterical fit of laughter after he noticed his foot was bleeding from some rock in the lake. My mom said it was one of those laugh-or-cry days. Then we all started laughing until our stomachs hurt.

There's a framed photo of the five of us on the mantel in my living room. We were standing next to the edge of the tiny pool, barefoot and holding ice-cream sandwiches and our stomachs, a feather floating in the background. It was the first time that I thought of all of us as a family.

My parents hadn't wanted me to know. They thought they could still keep things from me. But I knew Nick better than anyone. I knew he'd be waiting at my house the first night I was home from the hospital.

"Where is he?" I'd asked.

"We haven't heard from him," my dad had said.

But his look had said something else. He had forgotten that I knew what his face looked like when Nick was in trouble.

"What happened?"

They'd traded looks and then my mom had pulled out a kitchen chair.

"Sit down, baby," she'd said.

It'd only been a couple weeks, but my mom was like a different person. She'd always been so driven and goal-oriented. Now her favorite thing to say when I couldn't make up my mind about something was "Don't worry. No need to stress," or "It's fine. We'll just take it day by day." Who was this person who no longer planned things out five years in advance?

She hid my mail from me. Earlier today, I had found three letters from different universities hidden behind the bread box.

I'd wanted to go back to school right away, but my parents had told me it would be good for me to take a break, said we'd see how I was feeling in a couple of weeks. I hated it. I'd never missed a day before. On the first day of Pre-K 4, the school secretary had asked me which Pre-K I was there for,

3 or 4, because I was small for my age. I remembered being upset, because I hadn't known there was a Pre-K 3. I'd felt wronged.

Now school would be over soon and I really wanted everything to go back to normal first. Dr. Keels had said that that was a dangerous train of thought, though, that there was no going back to normal. She'd said the challenge was finding a new normal. She'd also said I needed to avoid stress triggers, and my parents were worried that school was a land mine. Most of my classes were AP classes, so I didn't need them to graduate. It still felt like I was missing out, though. I didn't want people to think that I couldn't do the things I used to do, and I was eager to prove to my parents that I could handle school and my symptoms at the same time. I didn't know if it was true or not but I was ready to find out.

My mom opened my bedroom door to check on me. She checked on me a lot. She saw the university letters sitting on my bed. I hadn't opened them.

"June, I just don't think it's a good idea to worry about college right now," she explained. "You have enough on your plate."

"I'm not worried about it. I just think it's weird that you'd hide them."

"I don't want you to s—"

"Stress, I know. I don't want to either, believe me, but I still have to pick one."

Her face changed. "Who says?"

"What do you mean?"

"Who says that you have to go to college right after high school? You can take some time off and focus on yourself."

I didn't know who I was talking to. This was the person who had dressed me in Brown University onesies as an infant. I was at least eight before I'd realized college was a choice. I'd thought it just came after twelfth grade, like twelfth came after eleventh.

"But I don't want to focus on me. I want to go to school and focus on something else."

I wanted to try on all the different Junes she'd been telling me about.

"I just don't see the rush," my mom said. She sat down next to me. "We have so much to figure out, to feel out, and it might be best to not put any extra demands on yourself."

She meant every word she said. I could tell. She truly thought that this was best for me. Maybe she was right. Maybe up was down and left was right and college didn't come after high school. Not for me. Not anymore.

"But what if the idea of not going to college stresses me out more than going?"

College had always been my path to something new. This felt like an avalanche. I was buried.

"I'm not saying never, June. I just think it's responsible to allow yourself a new timeline. There's nothing wrong with that."

Maybe a new timeline would be part of the new normal.

"Nothing has to be decided right now," she said. "I'm sure there's a compromise and we'll find it. I promise."

I wanted to believe her.

She left the room and I pulled out the information Dr. Keels had given me, the studies of people with schizophrenia who went to college and had jobs and spouses and kids. I opened my notebook to my list of occupations. Before, I couldn't decide on a major, and now the problem was compounded. It was one thing to think about managing my symptoms while going to college. It was another to think about the odds of getting a job after college. Would someone hire a teacher who heard voices?

I read all of the names in the studies and looked at the data tables with charts of hundreds of people, and they were each able to find a way. They each picked a path, chose a school, got a job. I reread each occupation on my list.

Dr. Keels would tell me to focus on one problem at a time, pick one obstacle and then tackle it. I was pretty sure my first obstacle would be convincing my parents that while we would have to find a new normal, with a new me, I still wanted the same things the old me did.

There was tapping on my window. Three soft taps letting me know it was Bethany. I lifted the window for her and she climbed in.

"You can use the front door now," I said.

"I like being sneaky. It makes everything more exciting."

She'd been at my house all evening, ever since I'd gotten home. I'd been officially released from the hospital. My mom had run her off eventually, when I started yawning, but Bethany had given me a look that had let me know she'd be back soon.

She plopped her bag down and opened it.

"I bought these," she said, pulling out headphones and handing them to me. "I meant to give them to you earlier but I forgot them at my house. They're noise-canceling. I read that they help drown out background noise, but you can use them to listen to music, too."

Background noise was code for *voices*. Dr. Keels had said headphones could be helpful in that department, just until the meds hit peak effect. I still had a week or so before that happened. And if my symptoms turned out to be persistent, the headphones might be a good long-term coping strategy.

"What did your dad say about Nick?" I asked.

Earlier, I'd sent Bethany home with a task: find out anything she could about what had happened to Nick. All my parents knew was that he'd been arrested for trying to steal a car and that he was being held at Durrant. My dad had called everyone he knew who might know something, but so far nothing.

"The only thing he knows is what was in the paper," she said.

I'd read the article online. I didn't know if I could trust what it said, though, because it'd called Nick a man. *A man was arrested for possession of a firearm and attempted grand theft auto in El Dorado.*

"He said nobody in town is talking about it," Bethany said. "Nobody at school is either." We sat down on my rug. "The timing couldn't be worse for this, but it's not good for you to worry about him," she added. "You need to focus on you."

"You sound like my parents," I said.

"They're smart people," she answered. "So Mr. Glover freaked out during physics when he realized that Scott Roberts didn't even know Newton's laws," she said. "And I mean freaked out, the whole 'What am I doing with my life, you people don't listen to anything I say' freak-out, and then he wished us all good luck with our futures and walked out. Oh, and Brian Watkins got suspended for vandalizing the boys' bathroom, and Carla and Miguel broke up again."

Carla and Miguel had been breaking up since we were in the fourth grade. Each time got more dramatic.

"She threw chocolate milk in his face, right in the middle of the cafeteria," Bethany said.

She told me everything, every second that I'd missed, because she knew I'd want to know all of it.

All our lives, the two of us had been a *we*. We had plans. We were going to college together. I didn't know how to tell her that I might not be going, at least not right away. Everything was different now and I didn't know what was in store for me.

"This doesn't change anything," Bethany said, reading my mind.

"Except that it changes everything," I countered.

"Don't do that. Don't start making lists of all the ways your life is screwed. We still get to have what we've always wanted."

"You do," I said. "You can still do all the things you've always wanted to do."

"So can you," she said. "It'll just be harder to do it. You've always worked hard, though. You can do this. You can handle whatever happens. Your future will look different, but it's still a future and you're still in it."

I loved her.

"I love you, too," she said, reading my mind again. "You look sleepy, June. It's a good look on you. Come on," she said, standing.

She pulled me up and led me to my bed. We slid under the covers, Bethany smoothing them over us. We stared at the ceiling.

"This is hard," I said. "Figuring out a new me, a new path. I didn't plan for this. I don't know what comes next."

"None of us do," she said. "Life is weird, June. There's only surprises."

She rolled toward me and scooted closer.

"Remember the time we went for a drive and saw that toilet on the side of the road and we stopped?" she asked.

"That's not something easily forgotten," I said.

"Yes. And it was brand-new! I still can't believe someone had thrown away a perfectly good toilet. And Nick picked it up and put it in the back of my truck because you can't just walk away from something like that."

It was last year and it was the middle of the night. We'd snuck out so Bethany could practice driving. The only time Bethany had felt comfortable driving was at night, when everyone was asleep and the roads were empty. It was Nick who had taught her how, because her parents weren't known for their patience and Bethany wasn't known for good driving.

"Nick said we should drop it off at school, but you wanted to keep it, because you'd seen something on Pinterest where people had flowers growing out of them," she said, and laughed.

"My dad did not appreciate it."

"But your mom did. She said it was so tacky that it was perfect and she grew, like, a thousand petunias out of it."

We still had it. The flowers looked more like a bush now, so it was hard to tell that the planter was a toilet.

"Why are we talking about this?" I asked.

"Because you forgot that something beautiful can grow from someplace unexpected."

"Wait—I'm the flowers in this analogy, right?"

"No, June," she said, exasperated. "You're the toilet."

We laughed so hard we shook the bed. My bedroom door opened.

"Bethany, get out of that bed and go home," my mom said.

She wasn't kidding. She was mad. She pointed to the window. Apparently Bethany wasn't allowed to use the front door anymore.

"No, please," I said. "I missed her and I feel more like myself when she's around. Please? Just for a little while longer." She had to see that Bethany was the best medicine.

She looked like she wasn't going to change her mind, but then she relented. "Okay, June. But only for an hour. No longer. Dr. Keels said we really have to enforce bedtime."

She looked embarrassed then, because she'd said *bedtime* like I was a little kid.

"It's okay, Mom. I know it's important. Bethany won't stay too long."

Bethany crossed her heart in a promise and my mom exhaled one long, loud breath.

As soon as my mom shut the door, Bethany looked at me sternly and said, "Repeat after me: I am June Daniels and I can do anything."

"I am June Daniels and I can do anything."

She looked at me sideways, like she wasn't sure she believed me. "We'll keep working on it," she said. She flipped to her back. "Would you rather eat an uncooked grasshopper or a cooked cricket?"

"Cooked cricket. Would you rather go skinny-dipping or streaking?"

"Skinny-dipping," she said. "Swimming is always better than running."

We laughed, quieter now, not wanting to risk Bethany's

eviction. The laughter rolled out of us until we were still and it was quiet.

"Do you think he's okay?" I asked.

"I hope so," she said. "He has to be."

He had to be.

She reached for the headphones on the side table. "Let's try them out." She turned them on and placed them on my head. "They're synced to my phone for now."

She pulled her phone out of her pocket and started a song. I smiled. It was Avril Lavigne's "Here's to Never Growing Up," a song Bethany was convinced was still my favorite.

"I haven't liked this song since we were thirteen."

"You sing every word to this song every time it comes on the radio," she countered.

"It's not like I forgot the words."

"I can't believe this was ever your favorite song," she said.

"It was the eighth grade. It was a confusing time."

I held the headphones out and Bethany leaned in so she could hear. We sang together. Bethany knew all the words, too.

"Pick a different one," I said.

We listened to music and traded stories and had so many would-you-rather conversations, until we were sure that we had each uncovered unknown layers of the other person. Bethany stayed and stayed, late into the night, until she was sure that I remembered who I was.

I thought I heard my name. There was a feeling like some-one's fingers on my arm, sliding down and back up again. It was nice. I didn't want it to stop. When it did, I opened my eyes.

Nick was squatting next to my bed, his face so close to mine. His face was bathed in lamplight. I'd asked Bethany not to turn the lamp off when she left.

My brain was in a fog and I blinked a few times, trying to clear it. Since I'd started taking something to help me sleep, I hadn't woken up in the middle of the night. Maybe that was it. I wasn't awake. I was dreaming, because he couldn't be here.

"Hey," he whispered.

"Hey," I whispered back.

Dream Nick pushed my covers off and slid me over so he could get in the bed with me. He didn't take off his shoes.

We faced each other.

"I missed you," he said, pulling me into him.

His nose was cold where it pressed into my neck. His nose felt real. He felt real.

"It's so good to see you here and not in the hospital," he said, his voice muffled in my neck. "Are you feeling okay?"

I nodded, because I really didn't want to get into all of the particulars with Dream Nick.

He held me for a long time, his fingers drawing circles on my back just like real Nick did.

"Are you real?" I asked.

"I'm real," he said, pulling away from me so I could see his face.

My pajama shirt had risen up and his belt buckle pressed against the skin of my stomach. It was cold, too. My hands went to it. The metal felt real. His skin felt real.

"How are you here right now?" I asked.

"Some things happened," he said.

"What things?" I asked, untangling from him and sitting up, still trying to shake the fuzzy feeling in my brain. If this was real Nick, I needed to be sitting up.

"I left Durrant," he said, sitting up now, too.

"You were released?"

That would explain why he was here. He'd been released and he was so excited to see me that he couldn't wait until morning. He'd come straight over. But his face didn't look excited.

"I wasn't released. I broke out."

"What? Why would you do that? You're going to be in so much trouble."

"I had to."

"Why?"

"Because I'm leaving Creed," he said.

"To go where?"

I was surprisingly calm. Maybe that was the medication. He leaned over the side of the bed and pulled his backpack into the bed with us. Opening it, he pulled out a box. It was a Priority Mail box and it had the words *Cremated Remains* on the side.

"I'm going to Hank's."

He handed me the box. He couldn't be going to Hank's now. Who was inside the box? It couldn't be John. I hoped it wasn't John.

"Hank died," he said.

My hands cradled the box. "This is Hank?" I asked.

He nodded. "He had a heart attack."

"Why is he here?"

"My mom," he said. It was his only explanation.

He had tears in his eyes and I tried to hide the shock on my face. I'd seen him cry one other time and it was the night his dad had gone to prison.

"I'm so sorry, Nick," I said, leaning into him. I wanted to put my arms around him but I didn't think I should put Hank down yet.

He wiped his eyes. "And John's home. John was with him when it happened."

His eyes changed to something else. He wasn't sad anymore.

"I think something happened to him, too. Or something is going on with him. I don't know why he'd be home early. Why he wouldn't let me know that he was back."

He looked at me like he thought I might have an answer, but I couldn't know. I was just relieved John wasn't dead.

Nick got out of the bed and started pacing, back and forth, between my dresser and the window. He stopped and faced me.

"Let's get out of here," he said.

"You're always saying that to me."

"Because I always want to get out of here with you."

"I can't go anywhere. I have to stay here and deal with this. I can't run away."

He looked desperate. "It's not like before, when I'm gone a few months and then I'm home. They're trying me as an adult. It's five years or fifteen."

"What?"

"My lawyer said they're trying to crack down on Benny. I can tell them everything and get five years, or keep my mouth shut and take fifteen."

The air got sucked out of the room.

"I thought about taking five," he said. "You'd be done with school and I let myself think that maybe there'd be a way for us to be together, but then my aunt Linda came to see me and she told me about Hank and about John and . . . I have to go. I have to take Hank's ashes back and bury him. He never wanted to leave the mountain. And I have to see John. I need you to come with me. I don't think I can do this without you."

Five years.

He sat on the bed with me and took the box from my lap.

"I know I can't do this without you," he added.

He dropped his head like he was so tired.

"Tell me what to do and I'll do it," he said, resigned.

He meant it. He would do whatever I said, even if I told him to go back to Durrant.

"If you leave town, you'll be in even more trouble when you come back," I said.

He didn't say anything at first and then he nodded, his head still down. "That's why I'm not coming back."

"What?" I asked.

"I need you to come with me," he repeated. He looked into my eyes. I didn't know what he saw there, but he stood up, his face adamant. "Hear me out. You said you would come with me this summer, you—"

"But it's not the summer yet," I said.

"A lot has changed. I've had to move up the timeline."

He smiled, a small one, but this wasn't funny.

"I know it's not a good time," he said. "I didn't plan it like this and I know I'm asking a lot, but it's only a five-hour drive. We'll be there tomorrow. Please. I need you to do this with me."

His eyes begged me. He kept saying *need*.

"I'm not asking for forever. I don't deserve that. Just come with me to bury him. Then you can come back home."

"How am I getting back?"

"You can drive Hank's truck."

"I don't know how to drive."

"I'll teach you. You can do this. You can do anything."

Just like Bethany had said. This wasn't what she'd had in mind, though. I couldn't breathe.

"But you're not coming back? What will you do?"

"I'll take what I need from Hank's cabin and I'll head to mine and John's camping spot. Nobody knows where it is."

"You'll just disappear?" I asked. I was crying now.

His face changed and I could tell he was sorry.

"You lied to me," I said. "You told me you'd quit Benny's, but you stole another car and now . . . now . . ."

Now our lives would never be like they were supposed to be.

"I didn't lie. I did quit," he said, walking to me. "That was my last job. Benny said he'd pay extra for this car and I needed the money." He sat on the bed. "I was gonna tell you about it. I wanted to tell you about it," he said, reaching for my hand. "But I didn't want you to worry about me."

"That's not it," I said, pulling away from him. "You knew how angry I'd be. You didn't want me to be mad at you."

"No, I didn't want that either," he admitted. "I had plans. When we went to Hank's, I was gonna ask him if I could move up there with him."

He'd wanted to move up there.

"You and Bethany are going off somewhere and I know you think I can come with you and make a life anywhere, but that's not true."

He didn't know my plans had changed. He was squeezing my hand too tight.

"I can't see myself somewhere else. But when I'm in the Ozarks, there's a whole other side of me, and I wanted you to see it. I wanted you to see that you could live out there, too."

He'd wanted me to live out there, too.

He wouldn't look at me now, just kept holding my hand and staring at the floor. "Hank knows these people who live completely off the grid and they make it fine. They've been making it in the mountains for, like, generations. I wanted to do it, too, but I needed all the money I could get." He finally looked at me and his face was full of regret. "Everything I try to do turns to shit."

It was true. He never knew the right way to get what he wanted.

"I gotta get out of here," he said. "I have to bring Hank home. Will you come with me?"

He was going to start his adventure in the woods and I didn't know what I'd do, but I'd agree to most anything if it meant putting off saying goodbye to him. I didn't know if I could do it, but maybe I wouldn't need college to try on a different June. Maybe I could try one on now.

"Okay," I said.

Such a small word to change everything.

He didn't waste time, just went to the closet and threw the door open, not waiting for me to change my mind. His movements were hurried. "You'll need jeans. Maybe a jacket. It can still get cold at night this time of year. Do you have boots? You'll need boots."

He started throwing things in a bag he'd pulled from my closet. I knew I should move but I felt stuck, watching him pack for me.

"June? Are we doing this?" he asked when he noticed I hadn't started moving yet.

I thought about what Dr. Keels had said about how important it was to stick to my routine. But she couldn't know that

Nick's uncle would die and Nick would need me to go with him to bury his ashes.

"We're doing this," I said.

I got up and went to the bathroom and pulled on clothes. I grabbed my medication. We'd be at the cabin the next day, but I didn't know how long I was staying. Judging from the number of clothes Nick was stuffing in my bag, it'd be a few days. I didn't know how much medication I'd need, so I brought all of it.

Nick stood in the middle of the room, my bag in his hand. I dropped the meds in it and grabbed the headphones and notebook off my desk. I stuffed my feet in shoes and grabbed my cell phone.

"Leave it," Nick said. "They'll be able to track you."

My parents. What would they do when they found my bed empty in the morning?

I tore a page from my notebook and grabbed a pen from my desk and started writing.

Please understand. I'll be home soon. I love you.

I left the note on my bed and was almost to the window when I realized that my parents wouldn't get to tell Nick goodbye. I ran back to the bed and added *Nick loves you, too.*

We climbed down the ladder and ran to his car, except it wasn't his car. He led us to an older-model black car parked down the street, two houses down. Nick opened my door. My knight in a white T-shirt and scuffed-up Converse. His eyes said he was sorry for stealing another one.

"I can't take my car," he explained. "They'll be looking for it."

This car had a bench front seat like Nick's but no shoulder belts, my hand hanging in the air where a belt should've been. There was no belt in the seat either and I felt out of control.

"We're gonna be okay," he said, breathless from running.

But what if he was wrong? What if this made me sicker?

My hands shook with fear, or maybe it was excitement. We rode down the street, Uncle Hank sitting between us.

We were about to pass Bethany's house. She didn't live far from me. The light in her bedroom was on.

I opened my notebook and scribbled:

> Dear Bethany,
>> Forgive me for leaving without you.
>>> Love, June
>
> P.S. You were right. There are so many surprises.

Ripping the page out of the notebook, I rolled the window down and sent it flying, hoping she'd find it.

CHAPTER 12

The road was dark. There were no streetlamps on the route I was taking. It was only a five-hour drive if you took the easy way, but the way we were going wouldn't be easy and I was pretty sure this car wasn't going to make it very far. It was a bitch not having GPS. We had to avoid the interstate and major highways for obvious reasons, so I was doing a lot of guesswork when it came to deciding which way to go. There was a map in the glove compartment but it wasn't that useful. A lot of the back roads of Arkansas weren't on a map.

June was asleep, curled up on the seat, using my backpack as a pillow. She'd been trying to stay awake but her meds were too strong.

I couldn't believe Hank was dead. It felt like I'd slipped

into some alternate timeline and any minute I'd wake up and this would all be a bad dream. I kept replaying the last thing I'd said to him, and my eyes burned.

June shifted in the seat and frowned in her sleep like she was thinking about something she didn't like. I kept waiting to feel bad for bringing her with me, but so far I didn't. I didn't regret leaving juvie either. Breaking out hadn't been as easy as I'd hoped, though. I'd almost gotten caught when I slipped out of the kitchen. I hadn't counted on the guards that were making the rounds right outside. I darted to hide behind the trash cans and knocked into them, making noise. I held my breath for what felt like forever when I heard the guards stop. I could *feel* them looking at the trash cans. They must've figured it was a rat, because after a couple of seconds, they started walking again. I started breathing again.

Once I got to the truck, I hid in between crates. There were too many of them for me to have room to sit, so I crouched down the best I could. When the driver of the truck pulled the door closed, I was almost sure he saw me, but if he did, he didn't react. Maybe he'd known boys were stealing rides all along.

It took me almost two hours to walk from the food depot to the barn. Cutting through the woods to avoid being seen, I made it there an hour past dark. I hadn't expected Tommy to be there, figured he'd just drop my bag off and leave, but he was sleeping on the cot in the barn's loft, my bag next to him. I wanted to take it without waking him but then changed my mind. Just because goodbyes were hard didn't mean you shouldn't say them.

"Hey, Tommy," I said. "Wake up."

He opened his eyes slowly and then sat up all at once. "I didn't know how long it would take you," he said. "I didn't want to miss you."

"Thanks for doing this." I picked up my bag.

"No problem," he said. "It's all there."

I opened the backpack and pulled out the package. Rocks settled in my gut.

"By the way, that's gross, dude," Tommy said. "Who is it?"

"My uncle."

It was the first time me and Hank had been in the barn together. My legs felt funny and I had to sit down.

"Oh. Sorry, man." He sounded like he meant it. "You didn't hear because you were out of town, but I quit Benny's."

He made it sound like I'd taken a vacation.

"Really? Does Benny know about it?"

"I didn't write him a letter of resignation or anything, but I think he'll figure it out when I don't come back to the garage."

"What are you doing for money?" He was the sole provider at his house.

"My mom found work," he said. "She got a job at Bates Sawmill. She's the only woman on her shift." He smiled, proud of her.

"That's awesome, man."

"After what happened to you, she didn't want me working for Benny anymore. Said it was only a matter of time."

She was right.

"You're right to get out of there."

"I got you a going-away present," he said. "It's outside."

"I'll meet you out there." I needed a minute alone.

He nodded and climbed down the loft's ladder.

I lifted the mattress of the cot and grabbed the envelope hidden there. It had three hundred dollars in it, the only money I had left after giving Aunt Linda what was under my bed. I tried not to think about it being the last time I'd walk out of the barn. There were years of my work on the barn's walls. I'd painted everything I couldn't say out loud, all the things I'd wanted, spread in colors along the metal and wood.

I didn't see Tommy when I walked out of the barn, but then I heard him.

"Over here," he said.

He was standing proudly next to an old car, a classic, one I'd know anywhere.

"What did you do?" I asked.

"You needed a ride," he said, a shit-eating grin on his face.

"In this car?"

"It's not like you can drive your car out of town. The police impounded it after you were arrested."

The car was a 1956 Continental Mark II—"Benny's Baby," as we called it at the garage. Benny had won it in a poker game in Memphis. It was his prize possession, the car he'd used as collateral to open the garage, a car he kept in a special storage room off the main garage, like a trophy. We'd all taken shifts washing it and driving it around from time to time to keep up the maintenance.

I couldn't keep the smile off my face. I didn't feel bad about it. Benny owed me double.

"Don't get too excited," Tommy said. "You know as well as I do that this car has maybe a hundred miles left in it."

It wouldn't make it all the way to the cabin, but it would make a point.

"But I figure it's what he deserves," Tommy said.

It was definitely what he deserved, and I felt happy for the first time since leaving Durrant.

"You know this means you can't come back," he said. "Benny's gonna think it was you who took it from the garage. If you come back, he'll kill you."

He said it with a smile, but we both knew it was true.

"I'm not coming back."

I opened the heavy car door and dropped my bag inside.

"You've got a full tank."

"Thanks, Tommy. This is more than you should've done."

"You're welcome." He gestured to the barn. "This place is really cool. Do you mind if I come back out here?"

"No, I don't mind. Come out here all you want."

I liked the idea. I didn't want to think about the barn being empty.

We were just inside Fordyce, and Benny's car wasn't going to make it much farther. We'd only been on the road a couple of hours. I thought about pulling over, or finding some dead end somewhere and parking, but I worried that someone might think we needed help and stop, so I parked in the lot of a tiny strip mall. Sometimes it was best to hide in plain sight. The car was wheezing out its last breaths. I'd ignored the knocking in the engine for the last fifteen miles. I picked a spot closer to the main road and parked away from the buildings.

June woke up when the car stopped.

"Where are we?" she asked.

"Fordyce," I said, rolling down my window.

She did the same.

"This car didn't make it as far as I'd hoped," I said. "We'll have to spend the rest of the night here. We'll get a new one in the morning. We should be to Hank's by tomorrow afternoon."

"A new one?" she asked.

I looked at her warily, waiting for her to tell me that she wasn't stealing cars with me, that it was a line she wouldn't cross, and demand that I take her home. Instead she picked up the box of Hank's ashes and weighed it carefully in her hands before putting it back in my bag.

"Come here to me," she said.

She'd been saying that to me since we were ten years old, and I always listened. I scooted to the middle and she climbed in my lap, my arms going around her. She pushed my hair off my face and studied it, her face in a deep frown.

"You look tired," she said.

"I am."

She looked in the back seat. "I think we'll both fit."

We'd both fit. I didn't care if I had to sleep on my side with one leg hanging off. I'd make it work. I wasn't letting her go.

I locked the doors and we climbed in the back. We lined up, the front of my body pressing against the back of hers. She reached back for my hand and I gave it to her. She brought it to her face and flipped it over to look at my palm. She looked at it like she might find answers there. Then she laced her fingers with mine and brought them to her chest.

My mouth went to her neck and she shivered. She did it every time I kissed her there.

"Do you think John is okay?" I asked.

"I hope so," she said. "Did you try calling him?"

"A couple of times, but he didn't answer. The service up there is shitty, though, so there's a good chance he can't get a signal."

It was quiet for a long time. I wondered if she realized I was making excuses for him, but maybe she'd gone back to sleep.

"I'm sorry about your uncle," she whispered. "I really wanted to meet him."

I'd wanted that, too. I tried pulling her closer to me, but we were as close as we could get. She rolled over so she was facing me and I grabbed her hip to keep her from falling off the seat.

"I've been trying to wrap my head around everything. It's not sinking in," I said. "I've been trying to think of reasons that would explain why John's already back. Or why he didn't at least let me know what was going on. I don't understand why he didn't let me know that he's home. I—"

She covered my mouth with her hand. "It's late. Now isn't the time to start thinking about the things you don't understand," she said. She dropped her hand.

"When is the time?"

"In the morning, when you're not so tired. Close your eyes," she said.

I closed them.

She ran her fingers through my hair, slowly, over and over. The repetitive motion made my eyelids heavy. I wouldn't be able to stay awake much longer. I knew sleep was good, but it felt like wasted time.

"You can go to sleep," she said, her fingers still doing their magic. "I'll watch over you and keep you safe," she promised.

I thought about protesting, reminding her that she needed protecting, too. Instead my fingers drew slow circles on her hip until it got too hard to move and I slept.

CHAPTER 13

Dear Bethany,

It's the first day I'll spend without you. I'm
in a parking lot and across the street is a sign
that reads "Garbage Only No Trash" and I've
been sitting here for the last few minutes trying
to figure it out. Remember that time we were
going to gymnastics camp and we passed a sign
that said "Humps for 500 Yards" and we laughed
so hard you almost wet yourself? In related news,
I peed behind a bush this morning. That was a
first.

I need to go. Nick is waking up.

I miss you.

Love, June

I tore the page out of my notebook and folded it carefully before putting it in my pocket.

Nick sat up and rubbed his face. "You should've woken me up. How long have you been awake?"

"Just a little while," I lied. "What time is it?"

He shrugged and looked uncomfortable. "I don't have my cell phone and there's no clock in this car."

A car with no seat belts wouldn't have a clock. He looked out the window like there might be clues to the time outside somewhere. The parking lot had filled up. It had to be pretty late in the morning.

"I need to take my meds," I said. "And I need some water. Bad."

My mouth felt like it was full of cotton. I was constantly thirsty now, another side effect of the medication. I needed to be careful with that. Dr. Keels had said dehydration could happen easily.

"I'm going to need a lot of water," I added.

He nodded. His face was serious. "I'll get you water." He put his shoes on and reached in his bag and pulled out his wallet. "I'll go across the street to that gas station," he said, pointing. "Do you mind staying with our stuff?"

I shook my head.

"I'll be right back."

He got out and I watched him walk across the street and into the store. I climbed over the front seat. I couldn't shake the nervous feeling I had. It felt like we were on the edge of something important and I didn't know if we were ready for it.

Nick came back out in no time, his arms full of water bottles and a bag dangling from his wrist. When he got to the car, I opened the door for him.

"Thank you," I said, taking one of the water bottles.

I grabbed my medicine from my bag and pulled out a tablet and placed it on my tongue. I wasn't supposed to swallow or chew it. I had to let it dissolve. It had a metallic taste, like I was sucking on a penny. Closing my eyes, I counted to ten to give it enough time to completely dissolve and then chased it with half of the bottle of water. It felt like my mouth was waking back up.

He reached in the plastic bag and pulled out a couple of cinnamon buns. They were my favorite gas station food. He handed me one.

"I didn't know if you could take your medicine on an empty stomach and I thought you might be hungry anyway."

"Thank you," I said, taking it from him and opening the wrapper. "What do we do now?" I asked.

His eyes scanned the parking lot, like he was deciding which car we'd steal. My heartbeat sped up. I was going to be no use to us if I was already scared. I tried to think of it not as a crime but as something that was necessary so that we could get Hank back to his cabin. Extreme times called for extreme measures. I'd read that somewhere.

"There's a neighborhood behind the shopping center," Nick said. "I saw it when we pulled in last night."

"Not one of these?" I asked, pointing to the cars around us.

He shook his head. "It's a bad idea to steal a car from a parking lot. The owner could be back at any minute."

We ate and then gathered all of our things, stuffing the water bottles into our bags, some in his, some in mine, and making sure Hank was secure. The front pocket of Nick's bag was open and I saw pictures of us. Bethany had taken them in the barn. He saw me notice them.

"I wanted something to look at," he said.

Because he wasn't coming back. Because this was one long goodbye.

We got out of the car and walked to the houses behind the line of stores, leaving the first stolen car I'd ever ridden in.

Nick took my hand and we walked down the sidewalk like it was a normal day and we were normal people. There was a NEIGHBORHOOD WATCH sign posted in the first front yard we passed and I wondered which house had the watcher. The street was lined with trees and there was a bench next to the sidewalk. As we walked by it, I pulled out Bethany's letter and dropped it there. Nick didn't see. If he did, he didn't say anything.

"Second cars are always a good option," he said. He gestured toward the driveways that had cars parked in them. "People don't usually notice they're missing until they get home from work, and maybe it's just an Arkansas thing, but most people leave their keys in the car when they park at home."

I wanted to ask him what happened if the cars in the

driveways weren't actually left behind but were there because someone was still at home, but his face was hard and
didn't look open for questions. It was a look I'd never seen
him wear before. This was Car Thief Nick.

"We need something that can handle rough terrain," he
said.

There was a jeep, a couple of old trucks that made Bethany's
truck look new, and a Camry. We faced the jeep, coming to
the same conclusion.

We walked to the jeep and my hands started sweating.
Nick noticed, because he was still holding one.

"It's okay," he said. "I'll be quick. It'll be fine."

But his three arrests said otherwise.

He walked to the driver's-side door and tried the handle.
It was unlocked and I started breathing again. I ran around
to the passenger side and dropped down in the seat, shutting
the door as quietly as I could.

"Shit," he said.

"What?"

"No keys."

He started digging in his backpack, like maybe there was
a chance the keys were in there. I lowered the visor and the
keys dropped in my lap.

"Who knew I'd be good at this?" I asked.

Nick smiled, the first real one he'd had since we left my
house, and swiped them from my lap. The jeep roared to life,
his smile bigger now. Mine matched it. We drove out of the

neighborhood, my head spinning with how fast a life could change.

"How much gas is in it?" I asked.

"A little less than half a tank."

I wanted to ask him if he had enough money for gas but I was afraid he'd say no, and if we were going to rob gas stations, I didn't want to know about it yet.

We'd been on the road about an hour when Nick pulled off to the side.

"Are we already out of gas?" I asked.

"No, we should have enough to get us to Little Rock."

"Then what are we doing?"

"It's time for your driving lesson," he said.

"No, it's not time for that."

My hands were sweating just thinking about it. Nick looked like his mind was made up and I tried not to remember everything I knew about the dangers of driving.

"Nick, this is a really bad idea."

"It's now or never," he said.

"We're on a mountain," I said, pointing out the side of the jeep, in case he'd missed it. "There's only a flimsy guardrail keeping us from plummeting to our deaths. I don't think this should be my starter lesson."

"Once we get to Little Rock, the path we're taking isn't smooth. In some places you can't even call it a road. This is the best place for your first practice. You've got to be able to drive Hank's truck back home. This is important."

I didn't want to think about going home without him, living the rest of my life without him, but I said, "Okay."

That word again.

He hopped out of the jeep and we switched sides. He was excited. He'd wanted to teach me how to drive for a while now.

I scooted the seat up, moving slowly, giving him time to realize this was a mistake and stop me.

"The first thing you do is check your mirrors," he said.

He wasn't stopping me.

"Fix them so you can see out of them," he said. "This is an automatic, so we only have to worry about two pedals."

Thank God for small miracles.

"Go ahead and tap the brake," he said.

The jeep was still running. I pressed the brake down.

"Good." He scooted close to me. "Now shift it into drive." He looked behind us. "You've got it. Take your foot off the brake, slowly." His breath moved across my shoulder and the hairs on the back of my neck stood.

"Are you sure?" My breathing was heavy. The nervous feeling from earlier was back twofold. My tongue felt thick. I was the last person who should be driving this jeep.

"Yeah, I'm sure," he said. He put his hand over mine and shifted the car into drive. "Pull out onto the road. Give it some gas. Good. A little more." His hand touched my leg, pushing it down. "A little more gas. You've got this."

The road was narrow, with two lanes, and I gripped the

steering wheel, trying to remember if I was supposed to keep my hands at ten and two or nine and three. I couldn't remember what the manual had said was the best hand position. Even though I'd never planned on actually driving, I'd read the driver's manual a few times because it was always better to be informed.

A tan Suburban came around the corner. I was sure the road wasn't big enough for both of us. I felt dizzy.

"It's coming right for us," I said, my breaths too short. It felt like I was panting and I couldn't stop it.

"It's not coming for us," he said. His hand hovered over mine on the steering wheel. He was more in my seat than he was in his. "It's in its lane. Take deep breaths."

"I should pull over," I said. "Just until they pass."

"You can't pull over every time a car comes by. You'll never make it back home. Stay in your lane. You're doing good."

"But this road is so narrow. Ahhh . . ." It was coming closer. "I can't look."

"Look! You have to look," he said, his hand on the wheel now.

The Suburban flew by us, shaking the jeep.

"Oh my God. Oh my God."

"It's okay," he said. "You're doing fine. Don't slow down. Keep accelerating. That's it," he said as he lifted his hand from the wheel. "You're doing it. I knew you could. You're driving, June."

I was driving. This was something everyone did and now I

was doing it. I was pretty sure I was terrible at it but I wasn't going to let that get me down. Nick was proud of me. My breathing went back to normal. The view was amazing, a tiny, winding road surrounded by the green of the trees and the blue sky. It looked like one of Nick's paintings.

"I don't ever remember you not knowing how to drive," I said.

Nick was back in the driver's seat. I'd never gone past thirty-five miles per hour, not the speed you needed to be going when you had an uncle to bury.

"I don't remember not knowing how to drive either," he said. "I spent so much time in the garage with my dad. Cars are just a part of me."

"Will you miss them?" I asked. "When you're out there, in the wilderness, building your cabin."

He didn't say anything at first, like he was really thinking about it, and then, "No." He glanced over at me. "It's a love-hate relationship," he said. "I loved spending time with my dad and my brother in the garage, working on cars, building them. I hate what they came to mean for me."

Like the situation he was in now. We passed a sign that said we were fifteen miles from a place called Amelia's Diner and my stomach growled. I put my hands on it to shut it up.

It seemed like we were the only people on the road, passing a car only every few miles or so. Nick kept switching the channels on the radio but it was hard to pick up a station. He finally just turned it off.

"Tell me about the people who live out there, the ones who can help you," I said.

He sat up straighter in his seat, like he'd been waiting for an invitation to talk about them. "There are people who've lived out there their whole lives. Some of them have never been off the mountain. Hank told me and John that he's known some of them forever. I mean, he knew them."

Nick had done that from time to time since we'd left Creed. He'd talk about Hank like he was still alive and then he'd remember he wasn't.

He told me about the people. He described them like a network of families. A lot of them were actually related, generations of families who'd never left the mountain. They made their own rules and had their own traditions. Others were like Hank, people who stepped out of their lives and walked into the woods and never came back. They were completely self-sufficient.

"So they never have to leave," he said. He was excited, his speech animated. "They take care of each other. There was one guy who'd come by every summer to check in with Hank, to see if he needed anything. He had a list and it was his job to make sure people had what they needed. If they didn't, he tried to help them get it."

He emphasized the word *need*. There would be no frills.

"So there's no electricity?"

"Where I'm going, there's no grid," he said. "Some people, like Hank, have solar panels, but you have to be somewhere with cleared land for that to work. Otherwise the trees are too tall and too close together."

"So what do you do?"

He shrugged. "Electricity is not really something you need."

"What about water?"

"Hank has a well, a lot of them do, but others live near fresh water. There's a stream near where me and John camp."

The place where he wanted to make his home.

He explained the water purification system he'd have, like he'd paid attention in science class. I knew he hadn't, so he must've learned this from Hank or John.

"You have it all figured out," I said.

"Not really. I've just been thinking about it for a long time."

I tried not to let the hurt show on my face. All this time, I'd been trying to figure out how he would fit into my future, and he'd been planning one without me.

"I always wanted you to be a part of it," he said, reading my mind. "I just didn't know how it would work. I don't know how your dreams and mine fit together."

I didn't either. I didn't even know what my dreams were anymore, or how my illness affected them.

"Won't it take a long time to build a cabin?" I asked.

He nodded. "Something like that could take years." He said it like it wasn't a bad thing, like he hoped it might.

"What will you do in the meantime?"

"Hank has a couple of tents that are heavy-duty and huge. They have rooms. Hank knew people who lived in tents like that full-time, so they could move around when they wanted to."

"But you don't want to do that?" I asked.

"No," he said, "I want something permanent."

Ever since I'd known Nick, that was what he'd been looking for, something that was permanent.

"But you're not buying the land. Doesn't somebody own it? What if they tell you to move?"

"Nobody goes out there, not in the five years I've been camping out there, not in the almost forty that Hank lived there."

"What will you do for food?"

He shrugged. "Hunt, fish, forage."

He made it all seem possible, almost easy. The missing parts of him were beginning to fill in, those parts of him that lived with his uncle in the summers, the parts that he never showed in Creed. I was close to seeing all of him now. It was the information I didn't have and another reason I'd been looking forward to this summer. I was even more eager to get to the cabin now.

He turned the jeep into the parking lot of Amelia's Diner. Maybe he'd heard my stomach earlier.

He put the jeep in park. "Don't make eye contact with anyone in here," he said. "Don't look scared either. It's like what I said in the hospital. Act like you belong in the room and people won't question it."

He was a fugitive. I'd forgotten that. I didn't know what that made me.

Walking into the diner, I felt like my skin was electric. There was no other way to describe the pulsing feeling that was in sync with my heartbeat as we opened the door and the bell above it chimed. I told myself that these were normal feelings to have in this situation. Anyone would feel this way. These weren't symptoms.

There was only a handful of people inside and I didn't know if that was a good thing or a bad thing. Nick touched my elbow and I jumped, squeaking out a "What?"

"Let's take this table," he said. His voice was extra calm, like he was trying to balance out my nervousness.

We sat and a waitress was at the table in seconds, handing us menus.

"What can I get for y'all?" she asked. Her head pointed down at her ticket pad, her pencil was at the ready. She looked like she'd stepped out of a casting call for diner waitresses.

"I'll have the burger, well done, with fries," Nick said.

"And I'll have the blueberry pancakes."

It was one of those diners where you could get breakfast all day. Breakfast food was my favorite kind of food.

She scribbled on her pad and took the menus back. "It'll be out soon," she said, and walked back to the kitchen.

Reaching into his backpack, Nick pulled out a pen and

then grabbed a napkin and started drawing on it. I didn't give it much thought at first. He finished and presented it to me.

"What is this?" I asked.

"Your driver's license."

He'd drawn my face in the center of the napkin and he'd written *Arkansas* across the top and it had my address, and yes, I was an organ donor.

"Is this valid?" I asked, taking it from him.

"Of course it is. Just sign right here." He pointed to the bottom of the napkin.

I took the pen from him and signed my name.

"You are officially qualified to drive any car I steal."

"Are you sure?" I asked. "I closed my eyes every time a car passed."

"Let's not forget when you took your hands off the wheel," he said, and laughed. "But these are things we can work on."

I folded it and put it in my pants pocket. It was a Nick original and I'd take very good care of it.

Our food arrived and we became silent. The diner had emptied out even more and now I could hear the sound of the television that hung above the counter.

"I've gotta go to the bathroom," Nick said. He pulled money out of his bag and put it on the table. "In case she comes back."

Across from our table was a woman sitting with her baby. She was making all these faces at the baby. The baby looked at the mom like there was nothing better in the world to look at. There were photos in my baby book of me looking at my mom just like that. My stomach hurt, thinking about my mom when she couldn't find me.

I wondered what my parents were doing right now. They'd probably pulled Bethany from her bed, sure that she'd know where Nick and I were headed, but Bethany wouldn't have had any clues to give them. They'd be panicked, sick with it. I was a terrible daughter.

There were two older men sitting in the booth next to the mom and baby. One stared at me like he knew me, but he couldn't know me. I didn't get out of Creed much and he'd never been to Creed. I knew all of Creed's faces.

The baby was laughing now and I couldn't stop watching her. The mom noticed. She didn't like me looking at her baby. I could tell. I didn't blame her.

There was something wrong with the TV, because it started making this high-pitched sound. I looked around the room to see if it was bothering anyone else, but they didn't seem to notice.

I didn't want to look at the mother anymore, because she made me sad. My parents would be okay, because they were parents. Nick needed me more than they did right now. I'd help Nick bury Hank and then I'd go back home. That hurt my stomach, too, though, because I'd be going home alone.

The waitress came by and I stopped her. "Can you change the channel on the TV? There's something wrong with that station."

She looked from me to the TV and frowned.

"Please," I added. The noise hurt my ears now.

"Sure," she said.

We'd bury Hank and I'd say goodbye to Nick, even though I couldn't imagine it. Then I'd drive Hank's truck back home, even though I couldn't imagine that either.

My hands were sweating again and my throat was tight and dry, like it was filling up with cotton. I raised my hand to get the waitress's attention. She was at the table in a second. She was good.

"Can I have some more water?"

She filled my glass and I emptied it right away. That was a little better.

I studied the men more closely now. They leaned into each other as they spoke. They had a way about them that was practiced. This diner wasn't a random destination for them but a plan. They knew what they were going to order before they got here, because it was always the same thing. They'd been coming here forever. I had to look away from them, because they made me sad, too.

Nick and I had never promised each other forever, never promised that we'd be meeting at a diner in thirty years and ordering "the usual," but I think it was implied. I dug into Nick's backpack, searching. I'd seen his pocketknife in it earlier. I found it in the front zippered pocket. I picked out a tiny spot in the corner of the table that I didn't think anyone would notice and I carved my promise to Nick on the tabletop, even though I didn't know how we would make it come true. It didn't matter, though. When things didn't work out like you wanted, it didn't change how you felt. Forever became something else, nothing promised in real time, but a deal made with your hearts.

Nick came out of the bathroom and motioned for me to meet him at the front door of the diner. I dropped the pocket-knife back into the bag and slung it over my shoulder, walking fast now, leaving my words behind.

N + J forever.

CHAPTER 14

June had been hiding her face from me since we'd left the diner, pretending to be interested in whatever was happening out the passenger-side window. She didn't want me to know that she was crying. It was only a tear or two but I caught her wiping them away. When June was sad, it felt like rocks were in my gut and I didn't want to do anything but get them out.

"Talk to me," I said.

Nothing.

I told myself to drive slowly, like there wasn't anything wrong. I couldn't drive like we were running from something, and getting to Little Rock faster wouldn't fix whatever was going on with June.

"What happened when I was in the bathroom?"

Still nothing.

"June, please—"

"I'm fine. I just—" She flinched, her face going pale.

My stomach knotted, because I'd seen her do that a hundred times in the last few months. I knew what it meant. She pulled her notebook from her bag and started writing.

"What time is it?" she asked.

I glanced at the dashboard. "It's 1:32. Will you tell me what happened?" I asked.

"Yes," she said.

But she didn't stop writing.

We drove into Little Rock, the afternoon sun beating into the jeep. Little Rock was the closest Arkansas got to a big city. The traffic was bad, more so than usual.

The only time I ever came here was when I was on my way to the cabin. Most of Uncle Hank's art supplies came from here. He had a friend named Charlie who I always came to see before going up the mountain. Charlie lived in downtown Little Rock and was one of those people who could get you anything you needed. I wouldn't be seeing him this time, though.

The jeep was almost out of gas. Cars lined the streets and people were everywhere.

"It's the Downtown River Jam," June said, pointing at a sign as we passed it.

All along the river, tents were set up, selling crafts, jewelry, food. I pulled the jeep into a grocery store parking lot because I was scared it would run out of gas soon.

June seemed to be doing better now. She'd stopped crying and writing in her notebook. She still hadn't told me what had happened in the diner to upset her. She was on her third bottle of water. I'd have to get more soon.

"Do you have enough money for gas?" she asked.

"Yeah, but it's a better idea to switch cars. I need to be careful what I spend my money on. Besides, the owners of this one could've reported it stolen by now."

She looked sick to her stomach, like she really wasn't down with stealing two cars in one day. I didn't know what other options we had. Everything was out of control and I couldn't stop it. The only thing I knew to do was keep moving forward.

We got out of the jeep and set out on foot. The festival was in full swing. We passed a vendor selling clothes and there were dresses hanging from the top of the tent. The wind blew them like flags. There was a yellow one and it caught June's eye.

I wanted this to be the road trip that I'd planned. School would be out and we'd head for Hank's cabin. We wouldn't be running and he wouldn't be dead. I'd buy the yellow dress for June and we'd stop by the river and talk about a future that had both of us in it.

But I was used to not getting what I wanted.

The festival had attracted a lot of people, which was good since there were a lot of vehicles to choose from, but there was also a lot of security. Cops were on every street corner and June jumped every time she saw one.

"We can't take a car from this area," I said. "We need to go somewhere more secluded."

I tried to remember how to get to Charlie's from there. His neighborhood would be perfect. I knew it was close by.

We had made it a few blocks when June pulled me to a stop.

"Wait," she said. "I need a minute." She rubbed her hands across her face like she was trying to rub something away. "I don't think my meds are working. I don't think I have the right dosage. I need to talk to Dr. Keels, but I can't."

She dropped her head and took deep breaths, her shoulders rising and falling, and when she looked up at me, she looked lost—like even though she was standing right in front of me, she couldn't remember why. I pulled her to me, her face close to mine, and lowered my mouth to hers. She couldn't talk to Dr. Keels yet, but I could help her.

This was a reminding kiss. I brought her even closer, reminding her where I fit. Her fingers gripped my hips, telling me she remembered.

"You can do this, June," I said, pulling away from her. "We're gonna be okay." I hoped we would be. "We'll get another car and we'll get out of here. Nobody is gonna stop us. Tell me you believe me."

"I believe you," she said, but her eyes told a different story.

Someone passed by us too close and brushed against her. She flinched like it hurt, her hands fisting at her sides. We needed to keep moving. We circled back to the tent with the yellow dress. She noticed it again and I wanted her to have it. Maybe it would be the thing that made her feel better.

"Stay here," I said. "I'll be right back."

The woman in the tent turned away from me, talking to someone else, and I slid the yellow dress off its hanger. June would love the gift, even though it was stolen, even though I was a thief. But when I turned around, there was no June, only an empty space on the grass where June should have been.

CHAPTER 15

When I was a little girl, Bethany and Becky would come over and we'd play with dolls that my mom had handed down to me. They were the kind with eyes that closed when you leaned them back. We'd dress them up in different outfits, brush their hair, and give them names like Cara and Anna Belle. We'd practice being the best kind of mothers. Becky never wanted to stop playing, always holding her doll a little longer.

Your mind is not your own.

It was a whisper carried on the wind, and I turned my face, trying to catch it. The little girl's voice was back. She'd been whispering since we left the diner and I was scared she wouldn't go away this time. Was I taking the wrong dosage? Maybe I should take another pill, but I was scared to do that without Dr. Keels's permission. It was the stress. Dr. Keels had said stress could make my symptoms harder to manage.

Your mind is not your own, she said again. There was something in her voice that I recognized.

Guilt never really went away; it just lay dormant from time to time, until you were least expecting it. Then it could pop up, reminding you it still existed. Becky had never said what was happening to her out loud. That was my excuse to pretend that she was okay and that I was still a good person and a good friend. She didn't leave a note, just left us all behind. I knew she was never coming back. And now she was standing there on the street, her back to me.

This time I was sure it was her. This wasn't like that day when I was walking to school and saw her. Relief flooded me. Becky was okay. Maybe she'd been in Little Rock this whole time.

The street was so crowded. I didn't know where all the people had come from. Apparently the Downtown River Jam was popular, because there were so many people standing between me and her. I couldn't get to her.

"Becky," I called out.

She turned her head like she might've heard me but she didn't stop, only picked up her pace.

"Becky," I said, louder. Just a few more feet.

Becky doesn't want to see you, the little girl's voice said.

"She does," I said.

She knows you knew what he was doing to her and you didn't do anything about it.

"I didn't know for sure."

Becky never said it out loud.

"She'll forgive me."

The people mixing on the sidewalks made it harder to move. I bumped into a man and he looked at me like he knew me, like the man in the diner had. Did I know him? His face wasn't one I'd seen before. There was no time to figure it out, because Becky was getting away.

I pushed away from him. "Becky!" I yelled.

Was that Nick yelling back?

"Becky!" I yelled again.

Becky didn't stop. Maybe I was wrong and she couldn't hear me. Other people did, though, because they turned to look at me. They looked worried and backed away, giving me space on the sidewalk. Thank God, because now I could move faster.

"Becky!"

Maybe if I ran. It felt good to run.

"Becky!"

The sidewalk was uneven and I tripped, falling hard, the concrete rushing up to my face.

"Are you okay? Can I help you?" a man asked.

I'd skinned my palms and they bled. The man reached for me, taking my hand to help me up, but I jerked back. Becky was moving farther from me.

"Becky!" I yelled. "Did you see her?" I asked the man.

He didn't answer, just looked confused. I got up from the ground, my hands stinging.

"Becky!"

She didn't turn back, didn't stop. She couldn't hear me. It was the music and all the noise. Or the little girl was right and Becky couldn't forgive me.

"Becky!" I screamed, louder this time. My throat burned from it. My voice cracked.

Once, I'd tried giving her the doll, but she'd looked at me like the idea was crazy, like her house was no place for dolls.

"June!"

It was Nick. His voice came from behind and I wanted to turn to him but I couldn't risk taking my eyes off her. If I did, she might disappear. He was close to me now and out of breath, like he'd been running. Maybe he saw Becky, too, and wanted to help me.

He was at my back, his panted breaths on my neck, his fingers touching me softly, catching the blood dripping from my hands now.

"June," he said again, his voice so quiet.

Nick turned me slowly, like he thought fast movements might scare me away. His eyes were soft and saying *It's okay,* one of his hands was raised like he was praying that it was okay, his voice said, "It's okay."

His eyes darted around, looking at all the people. They formed a circle around us now.

"June," he repeated, like he was making sure it was me.

I nodded. I was June.

"It's Becky," I said, pointing in the direction that she'd gone. "She's here. In Little Rock. I saw her."

He might've believed me, but he didn't look away from my face. Maybe he thought I'd disappear if he took his eyes off me, like I'd thought Becky might. I couldn't see her anymore.

"She's real this time," I said. One look at him kept me talking. "I know how it sounds, but I saw her. She's been in Little Rock. She's okay."

There was a crowd now. We were fish in a bowl and the people watched us. There were police officers standing at the end of the street and someone was talking to one and pointed in our direction. Nick saw and squeezed my hand that he was still holding.

My eyes burned with tears, because Becky had disappeared, just like that day when I'd followed her behind her house.

If my mind wasn't my own, then I didn't know who it belonged to.

Nick squeezed my hand again. "You ready?" he asked.

I knew what he was asking and squeezed back twice. We ran like our lives depended on it, because they did.

Everyone darted out of our way. We turned a corner and ran down the street. The neighborhood was full of tiny shotgun houses that all looked the same, some of them run-down with boarded-up windows. Nick led us to a truck sitting in someone's driveway. He grabbed the handle and pulled, but it was locked.

"Shit," he said. He was sweating.

He let go of my hand and jumped in the back of the truck. There were tools scattered in the bed. He grabbed a crowbar, lifted, and swung. It crashed through the back window, the glass shattering and flying in different directions. I screamed but I couldn't hear it over the sound of blood rushing in my ears. Nick was inside the truck and had it cranked in seconds. He threw the passenger door open.

"It's important to avoid stress," Dr. Keels had said. She'd even written it in her notes, right under *Drink plenty of water while taking your medication.*

We were in the truck and flying down the street. Nick wore another new face, but I didn't have a name for it. He sped up, faster now. I looked for cops and listened for their sirens, because surely someone had heard the glass breaking or my screaming. Surely someone had noticed us flying away. My hands vibrated in my lap.

You're not crazy. You're sick, the little girl said.

I nodded my agreement.

We left Little Rock, Nick's fingers gripping the steering wheel, his knuckles white. I didn't know how far we'd gone when he looked at the dash and said, "We're not gonna make it very far before we run out of gas."

We were good at stealing vehicles that were low on gas. Nick sounded exhausted. We must have been crashing from the adrenaline rush, because my eyelids were heavy, too. He turned off the highway and down a county road before taking a right down a narrow path into the woods. He pulled the truck off to the side, farther into the trees, so we wouldn't be seen. The sun was setting.

My breathing was heavy, my hand on my chest, counting the beats of my heart. I knew it still beat too fast and I wondered about all the things that caused a heart attack. I pulled out my notebook and opened to a new page and titled it "A Heart Attack Feels Like This," but then I scratched it out and wrote "Becky Wilkes Is Okay." I couldn't write fast enough, listing all the ways that Becky was fine now. My handwriting looked like scratch marks.

Nick's arm brushed past me as he picked up his bag, but I couldn't be bothered by it. I needed to finish the list.

"June," he said.

He put his hand on mine so I'd have to look at him.

He held a yellow dress. It was like the one from the street festival. It had eyelet embroidery around the collar and the sleeves. I'd noticed it because it was like the dresses that old June had worn.

Nick held the dress out to me. His eyes were sad. "I wanted you to have something yellow," he explained.

He was trying to fix things, to fix me.

I took it from him. "Thank you."

He reached for my hands, turning them over in his. He studied the scratches on my palms like there might be a test later, but all he said was my name.

"June."

I waited for him to say more, but there was nothing.

The energy from the street festival had followed us into the truck. It was trapped here, even with the back window busted out. We breathed it, in and out. It made the hairs on my arms stand. It tickled my lips.

"I'm sorry," he said finally.

"For what?"

"I never should have—"

"Don't say it."

"I knew you weren't okay, but I didn't care." He looked angry now, but I knew it wasn't me he was mad at. "I just wanted you with me. I thought you'd be okay with me. I thought I could take care of you. That I could be all you needed again. I was so stupid."

"You're not stupid. I am okay with you."

He knew I was lying. He looked heartbroken. I'd broken his heart.

"I'll feel better soon," I promised. "I'm already feeling better."

He didn't believe me.

"Don't look at me like that," I said. I was mad now, too.

"Like what?"

"Like you're scared of me."

"I'm not scared of you." He swallowed and I watched his Adam's apple move up and down in his throat.

"Are you sure?"

He reached for me, pulling me across the seat to him. It was the saddest I'd ever seen him, sadder than when his dad went to prison and John was deployed, sadder than after his mom left town and he told me Hank was dead. He took the dress from me and laid it across the steering wheel. He surprised me by reaching for my shirt. He slid it over my head. We sat for stretched seconds as he looked at me like he did sometimes before he painted on me. He put his hand over my heart and his mouth moved, just a little. I leaned closer to him, to see if I could hear what he was saying. Our noses bumped and then our mouths met. Everything slowed down, our movements, time, before speeding back up, our breathing louder now. Arms and legs bumped the dash and the steering wheel as we shed our clothes in the tiny space.

"I'm not scared of you," he said again.

This time I believed him. Our movements were hurried and our hands were everywhere. The leather on the seat was split and the broken glass from the window had settled in the cracks, but it didn't cut us. If it did, it didn't hurt.

Our movements slowed down again. He pushed my hair off my face. His lips pressed against my shoulder. We moved slower and slower, until we were still, like someone had hit a pause button.

"I love you," he said.

Even if he was sorry for bringing me with him, he'd said those words, even if his voice was rough when he said them, like they'd been cut from his throat.

"I love you, too," I said.

His eyes stayed locked to mine as he started moving again. Under the canopy of trees, in the cab of a stolen truck, he looked at me like I was all he needed.

CHAPTER 16

The pinks filled in a little at a time as the sun pushed up between the trees. It looked like someone had a crayon and was coloring in the lines. I looked at my hands. There was no paint there. I hadn't touched paint in days.

June slept with her head in my lap. I'd watched her all night, only nodding off a time or two, too scared to take my eyes off her in case she disappeared again. She held her notebook to her chest like it was the thing keeping her safe. When she slept, it was easy to pretend that she was fine, that I wasn't a horrible person for bringing her with me. It was the most selfish thing I'd ever done and I had to make it right.

She shifted and then opened her eyes. "Hey, you," she said.

"Hey. We need to get going," I said.

She sat up and I grabbed our bags and opened the truck door. I had to make it right soon.

"We're not going in the truck?" she asked.

"We'll come back for it. There's somewhere else we gotta go this morning."

"And we're walking there?"

"Yeah, but not far."

We moved through the woods, trying to avoid the mud.

"Are you okay?" she asked.

I shook my head. Neither of us was.

We walked out of the woods and onto the path. In the morning light, June could tell that it was a driveway.

"Did we park in someone's yard last night?" she asked.

"Something like that," I said.

She looked at me, puzzled, and then the lightbulb came on when she realized that I knew exactly where we were.

We continued walking down the path until it opened up into a front yard. Sitting at the back of the property was a house trailer.

"Where are we?" she asked.

It was just a yard, but it felt like a battlefield I had to cross.

"My mom's," I said.

It'd been almost a year since I'd seen her, since the beginning of last summer when I was on my way to Hank's. I usually stopped in before heading up the mountain.

We stood side by side on the makeshift front porch of the trailer, my hand in the air like I was going to knock, but I didn't. June looked like she might do it for me. I had never told June much about my mom. Anytime June brought her up, I'd change the subject or act like it didn't bother me that she was gone. June knew better. She'd seen the photo of my mom that I kept in my wallet.

I didn't want to be here, but we needed help. And maybe part of me needed to say goodbye to my mom before I disappeared for good.

Dogs barked from inside the trailer. The floor creaked as someone moved around. I rapped my knuckles on the door and the movement from inside the trailer stopped. The footsteps sounded closer as whoever it was walked to the door. It felt like we were all holding our breath. There was the sound of the chain being unlocked and the door opened.

The person standing there was an older man with gray hair and tattoos on every part of his skin except for his face. If it wasn't for the tattoos, he'd look like that old guy in all the western movies my dad used to watch, the one who sounded like he'd been smoking since he was five.

The door squeaked in complaint as he pushed it all the way open.

"Hi, Larry," I said.

It was the man my mom had left me for.

"I can't say I'm surprised," he said.

"It's good to see you, too," I said. "This is June, my—"

"I know who she is," Larry said. "We've heard all about her. Y'all are all over the news."

That was a surprise. June looked like she was going to be sick.

"June, this is Larry, my mom's husband."

"She told you we got married?" he asked.

"No, Dad did. Congratulations."

He nodded.

"Is she here?"

"She's still in the bed," Larry said. "Y'all come in and I'll go wake her up."

The two dogs were excited that we were here and they jumped at our legs. June loved dogs and she bent down to pet them; they pounced on her, almost knocking her to the floor.

Larry came back in the living room. "She'll be just a minute," he said. "Why don't y'all have a seat at the table?"

It was a question, but he didn't say it like one, gesturing toward the kitchen table. I couldn't shake the feeling that I was in trouble. We each took a chair. Minutes ticked by before a door in the back of the trailer opened and footsteps could be heard coming down the hall.

"There he is."

My mom's voice was the same as it always was, raspy and quiet. She was wrapped in a ratty bathrobe. Her face was puffy with sleep. She looked directly at me.

I didn't say anything, didn't move. My anger leaked out of me like it always did when I was in a room with her. I hated it. I wanted to hold on to the anger, but the little boy in me was always quick to forgive her.

"Mom," I said. My voice sounded younger and I hated that, too. I cleared my throat. June put her hand on top of mine.

"It's good to see you, June," my mom said. "It's been a minute."

"It's good to see you, too," June said.

June didn't look like it was good, though. She looked mad. She looked like she was remembering all those nights I'd spent in her room after my mom had left town, before I'd gotten the courage to ask Aunt Linda if I could live with her.

"Get over here and give me a hug," she said.

I counted to three before I stood. I went to her and bent down so she could hug me. She held me and didn't let go right away.

"You've gotten so tall," she said.

I'd outgrown her a long time ago.

Larry acted like there wasn't anything unusual going on in the kitchen and stood to put food in the dogs' bowls, talking to them the whole time.

"Let's go, boys. It's time for breakfast," he said.

I pushed back from my mom. She flinched, a dejected look passing across her face, but it was only a flash.

"The police have already been by here," she said. "The sheriff says I'm supposed to let him know if I see you." The look on her face said I didn't have to worry about that. "They have a pretty good idea that you're going to Hank's, but they don't know where the cabin is."

I knew she wouldn't tell them that either. Only a handful of people knew where Hank's cabin was or how to get there.

"Sit back down," she said. "I'll make breakfast."

Larry sat on the recliner in the living room and turned on the TV. June turned her head to the noise.

Mom took out a skillet from a drawer and opened the refrigerator, pulling out a slab of bacon. She heated the large cast-iron skillet and started placing the slices of bacon inside.

June studied her like she was taking notes on how to cook bacon.

After a time, my mom said, "What are you doing, Nick? What's the plan?"

"I couldn't stay in Creed," I said. "They're cracking down on Benny and I was looking at fifteen years if I didn't help them get him." I cleared my throat again. "And then Aunt Linda came to see me in Durrant."

She flinched at the mention of Aunt Linda. Maybe it hurt to hear about the woman who had stayed to take care of me. My anger was back now. I welcomed it. "I couldn't just let Hank sit on her mantle. He never wanted to leave his place. Ever."

That last part was an accusation. It was time for the fight now. She turned to face me like she was ready for it.

"I didn't know what else to do," she said. "We got no money." She looked around at the trailer, like she was pointing out the evidence. "How am I paying for a funeral? The hospital wouldn't release his body to me. John and me tried to get them to. John said he'd take Hank's body back to the cabin and we'd bury him together, but there are rules, procedures the hospital had to follow. It was either donate his body or have him cremated. All the other options were too expensive. And then John . . . he didn't take it well."

Every time she said John's name, it stung. She was one more person who knew he was home, one more person who knew more than I did.

"Why did John come back early?"

She shook her head and put her arm out to rest against the counter, like just thinking about it made her tired. "You think I know? He doesn't talk to me, doesn't tell me anything. I wouldn't have known the boy was home if he hadn't been with Hank when it happened."

"Why mail his ashes? Why wouldn't you keep him here, with you?"

"I didn't know where John got off to and I figured if only one of us got to keep him, it should be you," she said.

She said it like she thought she was doing the right thing. Maybe she was.

"I didn't know you were gonna get arrested, or that any of this other shit was gonna happen," she said, flicking her hand toward June. She angrily flipped over the bacon in the skillet. "So you're bringing him back? That's what this is about?"

"I'm bringing him home," I said.

"But now you've brought all this trouble down on you. They're gonna throw the book at you when you go back to Creed."

"I'm not going back."

June bumped the leg of the table with her bag as she stood, knocking over the salt and pepper shakers.

"I need to go to the bathroom," she said.

My mom pointed in the direction of the bathroom and June quickly walked down the hall and shut the door behind her.

"Somebody's not happy about that," Mom said. "I don't blame her."

"What does it matter to you?" I asked. "You're here. You don't come to Creed anyway. I see you once a year on my way to the cabin. If that."

"Seeing you once a year is better than never seeing you again," she said.

"Isn't not knowing where I am better than knowing *exactly* where I am?" I asked.

She knew I meant prison. She looked pained. She didn't say anything else. A few minutes later, June came out of the bathroom. The bacon burned. We ate it anyway.

"They've blocked the roads going up the mountain," Larry said, gesturing toward the TV.

It was a newsbreak. A reporter said that police had set up roadblocks along all major highways. There was a number to call if anyone had any information. They said it was a manhunt.

I'd known that they'd be looking for me, that I couldn't just walk out of Durrant and it not be a big deal, but I hadn't counted on a manhunt. I hadn't thought they'd try that hard to find me as long as I left town. Once I was out of Creed, I wasn't their problem anymore.

June stood next to me, her eyes glued to the TV. It was

her. It had to be. Her parents wanted her back. Everybody did. The only reason the cops were pulling out all the stops was because June was with me. Everybody wanted her back.

"They probably feel like a roadblock is the best way to stop y'all," Mom said. "They know once you get up the mountain, the odds of them finding you aren't good. You're not gonna be able to drive up to Hank's."

"What about walking in?" I asked.

"That could work," she said. "I know Hank hiked from here to the cabin before. You'll need supplies. We need to take a look out in the storage room. I've probably got what you'll need. We'll see if we can find Hank's old compass, too."

She kept throwing out the word *we* like she was a part of this.

"You're at least a four- or five-hour hike to the cabin from here," she said. "Well, that's how long it took Hank." She said it like it'd probably take me a lot longer. "You'll need matches, batteries, bug spray . . ." She moved around the kitchen and wrote everything down as it came to her.

June was still glued to the TV. She looked as shocked as I felt.

My mom came in the living room. "Let's go take a look," she said. She opened the back door and went outside, not waiting for us.

We followed her to the storage room out back and Mom starting handing me things.

"There's an old tent in here somewhere," she said. She

looked at June and then at me. "In case you don't make it to Hank's before nightfall." She pulled out an old army rucksack. "This was Hank's," she said. "He won't mind if you use it."

We packed everything she thought we'd need and I could carry into the rucksack. She found the compass. I'd need it for sure. I had a pretty good idea about the direction the cabin was in, but it was easy to get turned around out there.

June went inside for one more trip to the bathroom. She said it was because she wanted to take advantage of one while we had it, but I knew she wanted to give me a chance to be alone with my mom. I needed it.

My mom knew this was it. I wasn't coming back. She looked at me expectantly, like she needed me to say something to make all of this all right. When I didn't say anything, her shoulders slumped. I thought about what Hank used to tell me to do. He'd tell me to let go of the hurt and forgive her for not being the mom I needed. But that wasn't the hard part. He hadn't just wanted me to make peace with the bad times; he'd wanted me to try to remember things I didn't want to, the things it hurt to think about. He'd wanted me to remember the good times.

She put her arms around me for another hug. I hugged her back this time.

When I was seven years old, my mom had taken me and John to the county fair. She bought us blue cotton candy and we rode everything at least twice. The Ferris wheel was my favorite. She knew the guy working it and he let us ride it over and over again. We were some of the last people to leave, even though she had to get up early the next morning for work. On the way out, she held my hand and squeezed it three times. It was something she did from time to time. Each squeeze was a word. *I love you.*

I answered with two of my own squeezes, like she'd taught me. *How much?*

Then she pretend-squeezed my hand as hard as she could, grunting and putting on a real show.

"So much," she said.

I knew she loved me.

"I need you to do something else for me," I said now.

I could tell by the look on her face that she would agree to anything, and that was good, because that was what I needed.

June came back outside and I steeled myself. My mom didn't say anything, just walked back into the trailer.

June checked the gear. "There's only one sleeping bag," she said.

I nodded.

She raised her eyebrow, like she thought I was being cute, like I'd packed one so we'd have to share.

"You're not coming with me," I said.

"What?" Her face fell and my stomach fell with it.

"You're gonna stay with my mom and she'll call your parents. She's calling them now. They'll come get you."

"No." She looked back at the trailer, her face panicked.

"It's the right thing, June. I shouldn't have—"

"No," she repeated. "You don't get to do this."

"Do what?"

"Take it all away from me."

I reached for her but she backed away. I tried not to let the rejection show in my face. "June, last night—"

"I feel better."

She knew I didn't believe her.

"I promise," she said.

"It's too late." I gestured to the trailer.

"You asked me to come with you," she said. "You begged me. You said you needed me. You said you couldn't do it without me."

Because I was selfish.

"You said *need*. Is that not true anymore? You don't need me anymore?" she asked.

"Of course it's still true," I said. "But at what cost to you?"

"We can't stop now. We have to keep going. We're going to bury Hank and then you'll disappear and I'll never see you again."

"You were crying when we left that diner, like being with me was the wrong choice."

"That wasn't why I was crying."

"Then why—"

"We don't have time to get into everything that's led us here. We just have to do what we set out to do. That's the only thing we *can* do. You have to bury Hank. I have to be with you when you do it. I'll say goodbye to you there, not here in your mom's backyard."

Mom watched us through the tiny window in her back door. June followed my look to my mom and stood between us. She took my hand.

"Let's get out of here," she said. "I want to get out of here with you."

It was the only thing I wanted, too, even though it was a mistake. I squeezed her hand twice. I looked back at my mom and hoped that it wasn't too late, that she hadn't called June's parents yet.

"Let's go," I said, and pulled her into the woods.

CHAPTER 17

There was no path. There wasn't even a hint of one. I kept tripping, my feet catching on twigs and other things hidden in the underbrush. Nick didn't stumble. He walked easily, like the Ozarks were his backyard.

"I spy something green," I said, trying to lighten the mood. He hadn't said much since we'd left his mom's.

"Try spying something that isn't green," he said.

He wasn't mad at me, just worried. He didn't want to be wrong about bringing me with him.

"Is now a bad time to tell you I'm allergic to poison ivy, poison oak, pretty much all of the poisons?" I asked.

He'd been walking ahead of me and he turned to face me, walking backward.

"Show-off," I said, tripping over something sticking out of the ground.

"Since when are you allergic?" he asked.

"Since forever. Since the beginning of my life, or whenever it is you develop allergies."

"I can't believe I didn't know that," he said.

"You don't know everything about me. I have secrets."

"Like what?"

"If I told you, they wouldn't be secrets."

He smirked and turned back around.

There were some things he didn't need to know about, like the texts I'd just sent Bethany.

When I'd gone back inside his mom's trailer to use the bathroom, I'd seen Larry's cell phone on the edge of the kitchen table. I knew it was his because I'd seen him holding it earlier when he was watching TV. Larry was sitting in his recliner, his back to me, and I grabbed it and went to the bathroom and locked myself in. I shot a text to Bethany.

It's June. We're OK. Please tell my parents not to worry. Tell them I'm fine and to call off the manhunt. I'll be home soon.

I counted the seconds. By the time I got to thirty-two, I was convinced she wasn't going to text back, but then those three little dots popped up on the screen.

June!!! Where are you? It's too late to tell your parents not to worry. That ship has sailed. They've lost their minds. Are you really OK?

They'd lost their minds. But I knew that. There was a manhunt and roadblocks.

Yes, I'm OK.

We both knew that was a lie.

Please be careful. You've got to come back home.

I will.

When???

I didn't know when, so I didn't answer, just left the bathroom and put the cell phone back on the table. Larry hadn't moved and I was pretty sure I heard him snoring.

"What if the police come looking for us out here?" I asked Nick now, wanting to change the conversation and also because I was scared the police were coming in the woods after us.

He waved his arm out. "They can't sneak up on us out here. And they'll stick to the main trails. We won't be on those."

I'd noticed.

"Don't worry," Nick said. "We'll be fine."

But he looked nervous. He kept checking the compass and saying, "Don't worry," but he pushed us forward like we were running from something. If it wasn't the police, I wondered what we were running from. Maybe he was running *to* something. His uncle's place, his favorite spot, or John.

We'd walked miles and I was wilting. I knew Nick hoped we could make it to the cabin before dark. He'd check the compass and turn us this way or that way. I really hoped he knew how to read it and where we were going. For all I knew, we could've been walking in circles.

"We're not gonna make it to the cabin before nightfall," he said. "And we don't need to be walking out here in the dark. It's too easy to get turned around."

"Even with the compass?"

"Even with the compass."

We walked a bit farther and the ground leveled off. It seemed like we'd been on an incline since we'd left his mom's trailer.

"This is as good a spot as any," he said. "We'll camp here tonight." He dropped his pack and rolled his shoulders back. "I gotta use the bathroom," he said.

"Make sure you flush."

"Ha-ha. You're hilarious."

He stepped behind the trees and I pulled out my notebook.

I turned to a new page and titled it "Symptom-Free Days." Only a few more hours to go and I could add a tally mark. The little girl had been quiet all day. I'd thought about making a sign like the ones that hung outside the sawmills in Creed that read __ DAYS WITH NO ACCIDENTS. I was still debating it.

I turned to another page.

Dear Bethany,

I'm sorry I didn't text you back, but I don't know when this trip ends or when I'll be home. I'm camping without you for the first time. It'll be weird. We don't have flashlights or marshmallows.

I'm trying to focus on things that don't scare me. Yesterday we passed through a town called Flippin.

It's even smaller than Creed, just a mile along the highway, with only one church that I saw. It's the Flippin Church of God.

Love, June

I tore the page out, folded it in half, and placed it under a rock.

Nick was gone longer than I thought he should've been, so I set up the camp, pulling at the brush so we'd have a cleared spot for the tent. I didn't know how cold it would get at night, so I pulled out the jacket I knew Nick had packed for me and was unrolling the tent when he came back, his arms full of firewood.

"You're a natural," he said, smiling.

"This isn't my first camping trip."

"Yeah, but this isn't your backyard."

"That's true. Good thing I have you."

He let the wood drop to the ground and dug in his pack, pulling out matches. "Good thing," he said.

He had the tent up and the fire going in no time.

We sat across from each other, the fire between us, and we ate the only food we had. It was Little Debbie snack cakes and chips from his mom's pantry.

"Tell me another story," he said.

He wanted a distraction.

"What should it be about?" I asked.

"Tell me something that can't happen."

"Like what?"

Maybe he wanted another story with dragons.

"Tell me how we grow old together."

I met his eyes over the fire and saw the hurt in them.

"There was a girl named June and a boy named Nick," I said. "They lived on top of a mountain in a tiny cabin."

I tried to picture it. It would look like the cabin in Nick's painting, the one in the loft of the barn back in Creed.

"Nick spent his days trying to impress her, so she'd fall deeper and deeper in love with him."

"Did it work?" he asked.

"Yes. He built her something new every day and painted on her every night, and she loved him more than he thought she should, but he was wrong. She loved him just the right amount."

I wanted to come to his side of the fire but I stayed put.

"They lived out their days in the cabin, until they were old and gray," I said. "Until their wrinkles made them look nothing like they had before."

Until they'd said all the words that could be said, until there was only silence and the two of them.

"I wish it could be real," I said.

Nick didn't say anything, just threw a stick into the fire. And another one. And another one.

I stood and went to him, dropping down in front of him so he couldn't throw any more sticks in the fire.

"It's okay," I said, even though it wasn't.

He pulled me into his body, wrapping his arms around me, his face resting in the crook of my neck.

We heard the noise at the same time. I felt Nick tense up around me. It was the sound of twigs snapping under something heavy. My heartbeat picked up and I tried to remember what kinds of animals lived in the mountains.

Nick stood.

I was pretty sure that the Ozarks had bears.

The noise came from a gap between the trees, a thick black space, so black I couldn't see through it. This wasn't a symptom. There was something out there.

It came closer.

"Get in the tent," Nick said.

I stood to do what he said but it was too late. Nick pulled me behind him.

I saw the boots first. They stepped between the trees and into the clearing.

It wasn't a bear. It wasn't a symptom.

It was John.

CHAPTER 18

A round my uncle Hank's cabin, there were stands of yellow pine that reached ninety feet high and were so close together that they blocked out the sun. During my third summer at Hank's, I got lost. Earlier that day, me, Hank, and John had all set off to find a particular kind of birch wood that Hank needed for a project. Hank had thought we'd cover more ground if we split up, but he'd wanted me with either him or John, because he said I wasn't ready to go off on my own yet. I'd wanted to prove him wrong, so I agreed to go with John and then "accidentally" got separated from him. I'd always had a good sense of direction, so I thought I'd be fine. I'd show back up at Hank's and be like, "See, I told you I could do it. Now stop babying me."

What I'd forgotten about was that after you walked a

couple of hundred feet into the woods, the trees became a vacuum. They sucked everything in, even the light. It was impossible for me to get my bearings. One group of trees looked just like the rest, and I didn't know how to get back to the cabin. I remembered what Uncle Hank had said about the moss growing on the north side of the trees, but all of the trees around me had moss on all sides.

I didn't panic right away. Panic was something I knew I had to put off for as long as possible. When the sun started to set, I let go and started yelling. I yelled and yelled until I was hoarse. I was only making things worse by walking, so I stopped and sat down. I thought I'd die out there, until I heard John's voice. He yelled my name over and over again and I ran toward the sound.

I pushed through the trees and was out of breath when I got to him. He let out a long sigh of relief when he saw me. I was worried he'd be mad but he didn't say anything. He just gestured with his head for me to follow him and turned, leading me out of the dark. Neither of us could talk for days after that. We'd lost our voices yelling for each other.

John was standing right in front of me, but he didn't look like the John I'd left in the airport, or the guy in desert camo in the photo that he'd mailed with his letter. This John looked like the John in my dream, except there was no way he was dead, because June saw him, too. He looked like he'd been left outside too long. His face looked tan from so many days in the desert. I wondered if he hadn't been back long.

It was like that day I'd been lost in the woods, except the roles were reversed. It was John who'd gone rogue this time, who was somewhere he wasn't supposed to be. I knew I should be angry, but the relief in seeing him won out over everything else.

We didn't say anything, just stared at each other. If I was still a kid, I'd forgive him for not letting me know he was back and he'd tell me everything was going to be okay.

"What are you doing here?" he asked.

That was *my* line. I'd been gearing up to say it and now I had to think of what else to say. We were closer to each other, each moving to the other one.

"We're headed to Hank's."

He looked from me to June.

"It's a long story," I added.

By the look on his face, he had one of those, too. I was ready to hear it.

It was my turn now. "What are you doing here?"

He shrugged. "I was out for a walk and I heard y'all," he said.

But what are you doing here? I thought. "We're miles from Hank's," I said.

He shrugged again. "We're closer than you think, only a couple of miles, and I like to take walks at night," he said. "You know that."

We stood right in front of each other. I could reach out and touch him if I wanted.

He looked at our campsite, assessing.

"We're bringing Hank home," I said.

His eyes darted around like he expected Hank to walk out from between the trees. June ducked into the tent and came out with the box. John's eyes locked on it. He took a step toward June but then stopped. When he looked back at me, I saw a glimpse of the brother I'd left at the airport, but then he blinked and he was gone again.

He walked to the fire and sat down.

"Mom wouldn't listen to me," he said. "I told her not to mail him to Creed, that he'd want to stay out here, but she doesn't listen to anybody."

"How did it happen?" I asked. *How are you here right now?* I wanted to ask.

"The doctor said it was heart disease. He said Hank should've died a long time ago. I'd thought I'd caused it, but he said I couldn't have."

"Why did you think you caused it?" I sat next to him now.

"We'd been working from sunup to sundown," he said. "Hank knew I needed to stay busy. We were fixing the fence on the north side of the property. He wanted to replace all of the fence posts out there."

It was something he'd talked about doing last summer. I was supposed to help him with it.

"He sent me to his workshop to get a second ax, and when

I got back, he was on the ground." He shook his head, like he was trying to shake free from the memory. Then he stood. "Your fire's getting low," he said.

He bent down and picked up some sticks and branches, like this was a normal thing for him to do. He gathered the kindling and came closer, stoking the fire. His head turned to every sound coming from the forest.

"Have you eaten?" June asked.

We'd both forgotten that she was there. He shook his head, and she brought out the bag with the food and spread it out for him.

"As you can see, it's a cornucopia of goodness." Her voice was quiet, like she'd noticed how skittish he was and thought normal voice volumes would scare him off.

He grabbed a bag of Doritos.

We sat around the fire in silence. He knew what I was waiting for but he didn't say it. I wanted to hurl questions at him but he felt so different. It was awkward to throw questions at someone I didn't know.

I remembered what Aunt Linda had said about them having to pull him off Hank in the hospital. She'd said that John had gotten him there by himself. It was at least an hour to the nearest hospital from Uncle Hank's cabin if you were racing, which John probably had been. It had been an hour of him and a dying Uncle Hank alone in the cab of his truck. I shouldn't have been jealous, but I was. I wanted it to be me who'd been with him. I wanted to be the one who'd gotten that last hour.

He reached for another bag of chips, and I saw that his hands shook. He saw me notice and he put them in the pockets of his jacket.

He looked right at me for the first time since he'd walked out of the trees. "I can't shoot anymore," he said. "So they sent me home."

There was no more explanation. John got up and walked behind the tent, like he was inspecting how I set it up. Apparently he figured I did an okay job, because he said, "I'm gonna head back. You'll come to Hank's in the morning, right?"

It seemed we weren't invited to go back with him that night, so I nodded.

Looking at the box, he said, "We should bury him tomorrow. It's been too long already."

He turned and headed back the way he'd come.

"Wait," I said.

I'd wanted to see him for so long and I wasn't ready for our reunion to be over.

John faced me. He looked tired. It wasn't a normal kind of tired. His eyes looked like June's had right before she'd been admitted to the hospital. That kind of tired. "I'm glad you're home," I said. Even if him being home meant something terrible had happened.

"I'm glad you're home, too," he said. Because this place was always home.

He disappeared the same way he'd come, and I didn't know what else to do, so I just stared after him. Even though we were finally in the same place, I'd never felt farther from him.

Morning came early in the mountains and we started packing up our camp as soon as day broke. We'd slept like shit. June had woken with every noise. She'd tried to act like she wasn't scared, but I could tell she was. I'd told her I'd stay awake and keep a lookout.

We were getting close to the cabin now. I could see it in the distance and the workshop behind it and that spot on the hill where we'd bury him. I felt tears forming. I didn't know if it was the relief that Hank was back where he belonged or the sorrow that he was coming home as ashes.

The door to the workshop was open and I wondered if John was already out there working on something. When we were here, we spent more time in the workshop than we did in the cabin, using the cabin just to eat meals and sleep. The workshop was where me and John had really gotten to know Uncle Hank.

There was one night when me and Uncle Hank had been in the workshop, cleaning up. We'd been painting all day. There was a record player in the room. It was like the one we had in the barn. It was the only kind of sound system he ever owned. "Nothing beats vinyl," he'd say. He kept playing this one song over and over. It was Tommy James and the Shondells' "Crimson and Clover."

"This used to be my favorite song," he said.

He said *used to*, not *is* or *was*. He always looked back

on his life in Creed like it belonged to someone else, like he had a new life in the mountains, like he'd been reborn in the Ozarks. It was rare that he let his two lives share the same space. Over and over he played that song, until I'd memorized the words.

We were almost to the cabin's front door and I felt nervous, worried that I'd built it up in June's head and no way would the reality measure up. I tried seeing it through her eyes, worried about what she thought, but I shouldn't have worried. She looked at the cabin the same way she looked at the barn.

"It's just like you painted it," she said.

I pointed to the hill in the side yard that butted up to the woods on the far side of the property. "That's where we'll bury his ashes." Maybe once I'd done it, I'd be able to breathe easier.

We walked up to the front porch, the second step squeaking just like it was supposed to. Everything was like I'd left it. Except Uncle Hank wasn't inside. He wasn't in the workshop out back. My backpack felt heavier.

"Are you ready for your tour?" I asked, opening the door and trying to push back unwanted feelings. It wasn't locked. No need for that out here.

"Yes," she said.

I could tell she was excited and I led her into the living room. The last time I'd seen Hank had been in this room. We'd been fighting because he didn't want me working for Benny anymore. All summer he'd been trying to get me to promise to quit. He and June always gave me the same argument.

"There are better ways to make money," he said.

"Doing what? Working at one of the mills like you did? No thanks."

"Working at the mills won't get you sent to prison."

"Benny—"

"Doesn't give a shit about you. You are a way to make money and that's it. That's all your dad was to him and that's all you'll ever be to him."

I'd always known that was true, but it hurt and embarrassed me that Uncle Hank knew it, too.

"You come here every summer. And every summer I think you've finally gotten your head on right and then you go back home and do the same things that got you in trouble in the first place. How many times have you been arrested now?"

He didn't wait for my answer.

"You're not making any changes," he said. "You're just spinning your wheels."

"You don't know what my life is like," I said. "You only pretend to."

"That's not true. I know your life."

"It's easy to say that from out here, but you don't know Creed anymore."

"Tell yourself whatever you need to. Creed isn't as bad as you make it out to be."

"For people like us, it is. You ran away as soon as you got out of high school. You didn't even stop to take your stuff from the barn. You left. John did, too. God, Mom skipped town with the first guy who asked her to. She barely even knew Larry."

"Don't talk bad about your mom." He was always so quick to defend her.

"That's just your guilt talking because you know it's your fault she is the way she is."

"Shut up," he said.

"You didn't just leave Creed. You left her, too, and you *never* came back. You're the one that taught her how to leave her family. You're the one that showed her it was okay."

His face fell and I knew I'd gone too far.

"Do what you want, kid," he said, his voice quiet. "You're just like your dad."

"Fuck you."

It was the last thing I said to him.

And now he was gone and I couldn't make it right.

June walked down the hall, tiptoeing, probably to keep from waking John. I should've told her that no one ever woke up before John and that he was more than likely in the workshop.

A hall led to the bedrooms and a bathroom.

"This was my room when I was here," I said as I showed her the room.

The room was bare except for a bed in the center and

nightstands that I'd built. June didn't say anything, just went straight for the bed and crawled under the covers.

"It's the first bed I've seen since we left Creed," she said.

She curled on her side and closed her eyes. I didn't think she was asleep but she wasn't moving. I was about to join her when I heard the front door open.

I followed the sounds John made into the kitchen. He stood at the sink, looking out the window. The anger hit me suddenly. I was supposed to know him better than anyone. He'd said so right before he left. Now he was back home with shaking hands and I didn't know why and he didn't even care enough to tell me. I wanted to punch him. I took a step toward him. He turned to face me. He knew what I meant to do, because he squared off, like he was getting ready for it. It wouldn't be our first fight.

But I didn't hit him.

"What happened to you?" I asked instead.

He just stared at me.

"When you got sent home, you should've called me to let me know you were back. I could've come out here. I shouldn't have had to find out you were back the way I did."

I left the one question I couldn't ask hanging in the air.

Why didn't you want me to know?

"I'm sorry," he said. "Hank wanted me to tell you I was back, but I worried if I called, then you would come up here, and I wasn't ready to see anybody."

"I'm not *anybody*."

"I know that. I'm sorry," he said again.

"What happened to you?" I repeated.

He walked to the table in the center of the room and sat down in one of the chairs. I sat in another one.

"How's Tommy?" he asked.

"Good. He quit Benny's."

John looked surprised. "That *is* good. Uncle Hank had been filling me in on what's been going on with you."

Then he knew what an asshole I was. He knew how we'd left things.

"How's Aunt Linda?" he asked.

"She's good, too."

"Hank said she—"

"What happened to you?" I asked again.

We stared at each other. I wouldn't drop it and he knew it.

"I couldn't tell what day of the week it was," he said. "It's all the same. Every day. If it wasn't for the watches they made us wear, we'd never know the date or the time. I started to wonder if it was all a game, like a trick."

He leaned closer to me. "You know how mom used to set her clock in their bedroom ten minutes fast so she wouldn't be late for work?" he asked.

"Yeah."

"I worried that it might be like that, that the army set everybody's watches ahead, so we wouldn't know how much time had really passed. They kept saying we'd only been gone a few months, but it had to have been longer than that. It felt like it'd been years. I couldn't stop thinking about it, worrying about it. I don't know why. I just wanted to know if it was really Tuesday or not, you know?"

I didn't know.

"Nobody else was hung up on it. I tried to let it go and do what I was told."

He wasn't looking at me anymore. I'd noticed that he couldn't do that for very long. It was like he could only meet my eyes in short bursts and then he'd have to turn away. He was looking toward the window again.

"We had a routine inspection of an abandoned building," he said. "We did it at least once a day. There wasn't supposed to be anybody inside, much less a kid."

He met my eyes for two beats and then looked back toward the window.

"It was over before I knew what happened. I didn't even realize I'd fired my weapon."

I couldn't say anything, because what could be said. I tried to hide the emotion in my face.

"Everyone said that these things happen. That I was okay. That what I did was forgivable, but how can it be? He was just a kid. I couldn't let it go. I couldn't fire my gun anymore. I kept hesitating.

"I saw a doctor when I got back. She gave me meds. They've helped some." He put his hands on the table, pressing down so they didn't shake. "It's better if I stay busy." He looked around the room. "I gotta figure out who I am now. Hank was trying to help."

John needed someone to tell him what to do next. That was the difference I felt between this John and the one I'd left in the airport. This John didn't have a plan.

There was a deck of cards on the table. It was the only entertainment the cabin had to offer. I picked it up and shuffled it. Uncle Hank had taught us every card game imaginable. But we had a favorite.

I kept shuffling the cards. I didn't know what to tell John. I never knew the right next step, but I could deal cards.

"Wanna play Bullshit?" I asked.

He thought about it, and when I thought he was going to tell me no, he smiled.

"Sure," he said.

I dealt the cards and we played. We turned our brains off and let muscle memory take over, our hands knowing what to do. We played hand after hand, until we were laughing and John was standing and yelling, "Bullshit! There's no way you have those cards."

It was the best I'd felt in a long time and I could tell it was the same for him.

"Another hand?" I asked.

June came in the room, looking from me to John. We were loud. We must've woken her.

"Can I play?" she asked.

"Do you know how?" John asked.

"Nick taught me."

"Deal her in," he said to me.

I didn't know how many hands we'd played, but John started getting antsy, his eyes darting toward the window more and more. Finally, he put his cards down and pushed his chair back. The reprieve was over.

"I'll meet you on the hill," he said.

Hank kept his shovels behind the workshop. I grabbed one. I met June outside on the hill. She wore the yellow dress. She probably thought she should wear a dress since this was a funeral. She looked beautiful in it, just like I'd imagined she would.

John took the shovel from me and dug a couple of feet down. June gave me the box. It was lined with plastic and inside there was a wooden container that looked like one of Aunt Linda's jewelry boxes. It was wrapped in more packing material. I opened it. Uncle Hank's ashes were inside, sealed inside this bag that looked like a heavy-duty Ziploc.

I imagined Hank's face. I tried not to picture it like it had been the last time I saw him, hurt and disappointed. I hoped there was a heaven, so he'd be able to see that I'd brought him back home, so he'd forgive me.

I placed the box in the bottom of the hole.

I said the prayer that Hank taught us. "Dear Lord, we are grateful for your gifts."

I looked up and locked eyes with John.

"We are grateful for the trees you surround us with, that

protect and cloak us," John said with me. "We are grateful for the sky you hung above us and for your stars. Dear Lord, we are grateful for your gifts and we will always protect them, from now until the day we are returned to you. Amen."

That prayer was the only clue Hank had ever given us that he was spiritual, but he'd said it every time he killed an animal or cut down a tree. "It's important to show your gratitude," he'd say. Of all the things I was grateful for, I was most thankful for Hank.

We were quiet as I filled the hole with dirt. I felt better knowing that Hank was back where he belonged. I patted the dirt down with my hands.

June started to walk back to the cabin, and John sat down on the ground like he was exhausted, the air going out of him.

"I'll see you inside," I said to June.

I didn't know how to talk to John about what had happened to him and there were no cards out here, so I confessed my own sins.

"I got arrested again," I said.

He looked up at me, squinting his eyes against the sun. "Hank told me. I'm sorry I wasn't around for you."

I sat down next to him. "It's okay," I said. I'd always known I'd forgive him easily. I picked at the grass. "Hank didn't know about the last one, though."

He didn't say anything and he didn't look surprised.

"I got caught trying to steal a car in El Dorado. Benny wanted it. I knew it was a bad deal when I spotted the car.

It was right in the middle of downtown, but I did it anyway. Benny offered me more money and I convinced myself that I needed it."

There was no judgment coming from John. He only listened.

"They wanted to try me as an adult, because it was my third arrest and they found the gun in my glove compartment. That didn't help."

He leaned forward now and there was a look in his eyes that I recognized. The protective big brother was coming out in him. I kept talking so I could see more of him.

"They want Benny," I said. "The prosecutor offered me a deal. If I tell them everything I know, I'll get the minimum sentence."

"How long?" he asked.

"Five years."

His face said he couldn't believe it, but he quickly rearranged it.

"I was thinking about taking the time, but then Aunt Linda came to tell me about Hank and that you were home and . . . it felt like up was down. So I said screw it and waited for the food truck to come and I hid in the back."

"You broke out of Durrant?"

"I had to bring Hank home," I said.

And see you, I didn't say.

"What if you screwed up your deal?" he asked.

"I definitely screwed up my deal. But it doesn't matter."

"Why the hell not?"

"Because I'm not taking it. I'm not going back."

"You can't be serious," he said. He stood. He looked like I had when I'd walked in the kitchen earlier, like he was gearing up for a fight.

I stood, too. "I am serious," I said. "I'm not doing time for Benny."

"So you're gonna do what instead?"

I shrugged. "Go up the mountain." Start the life we'd been planning since we were kids.

"But you can put Benny away. You can be the one to stop him."

He almost sounded jealous.

I shook my head. "But five years? And that's if I get the minimum sentence. If not, I'll be in my thirties before I get out."

"I don't want that for you. You gotta believe me, but it's better than the alternative."

"How can it be better than this?" I asked, throwing my hands out to the sides, to the mountains around us.

He stepped closer to me. "Don't do this. The best parts of our childhood were out here. When we were kids, this place was our only escape. Don't let it become your prison."

He put his arm around my shoulder and I was ten years old again.

"Do you know how many guys are doing time because they got sucked in by Benny? He sets it up so you take all the risks and he keeps most of the money. And he makes you believe that he cares about you, that you're part of something bigger, like some screwed-up family, but it's not real. I'm your family," he said. "Hank was your family. And you're the best of us. So be the first one of us who doesn't run away. Take the deal. Tell them what they want to know. And when you get out, come back here on your own terms."

"No, I'm not doing that kind of time. I can't. Just a few months in Durrant and I felt like I was coming out of my skin, and you want me to go back so I can be locked up for years? No."

He started pacing. "I wanted it to be your choice," he said.

"What?"

"You were supposed to want to do the right thing."

"What are you talking about?"

"You're not disappearing," he said. "You're gonna do what's right." He was agitated. "The police are on their way here."

"What?" I had no words. I couldn't think.

"Mom called after you and June left her place," he explained. "She said y'all were headed here. That's why I was out in the woods last night. I was trying to find you. She told me what you planned to do. And I can't let you do it. I can't let you give up your whole life."

"You ratted me out?"

"It's not like that."

"What's it like, then?"

He didn't answer. I looked to the horizon, like I expected the police to appear at any moment.

"It'll be at least tomorrow morning before they make it out here," he said. "I told them how to get here, but not the easy way. I wanted to have more time with you."

He stepped closer but I backed up.

"One day you'll understand," he said. "I know you don't think so and you might hate me, but I had to do it. I promise you it's the right thing."

He looked around, studying the landscape, and then his eyes landed back on mine. "Hank always said we had to take care of each other. That's what I'm trying to do. You'll be okay. I'm gonna finish Hank's fence and then I'm gonna come see you. And Dad."

Because we'd be together.

"You don't get to decide what's right for me," I said. "Not anymore. You shouldn't have called the police. There are things you don't know."

I thought about June. I didn't know if the cops would descend with guns blazing or if it would be more civilized. I didn't know how she'd react or what would happen to her. There was too much I didn't know and all of it was out of my control. I couldn't believe that John had forced my hand, but it wasn't going down like that. I was through letting people make decisions for me.

"You're wrong," I said. "About everything."

I walked down the hill, away from him. He didn't follow.

June wasn't in the cabin. I had to find her and tell her what John had done. I couldn't be around when the police came. I walked around the back to the workshop. The door was open. The front room of the workshop was where Uncle Hank kept all of his woodwork projects. Different pieces of furniture sat in all stages of completion. These were pieces he'd never finish. Grieving was weird. It didn't hit me all at once like I'd thought it would, but a little bit at a time and when I least expected it. Though I wasn't grieving just Hank this time.

I found her in the back room, in his studio. She was studying all the pieces that hung around the space. She stared at the painting of Hank and my mom standing in front of that house they'd never lived in. She turned when she heard me. I'd miss her most of all, the girl I was never supposed to have.

She walked to the cot in the corner of the room and sat down. I felt torn in two pieces. Part of me wanted to run right then and part of me wanted to stay there with her. I went to the record player. Hank's record collection was varied. I flipped through the albums. I stopped when I found what I wanted.

It was Tommy James and the Shondells' "Crimson and Clover" and it played loud in the small space.

When I looked at June, she knew what I wanted, because she slid her shoes off and lifted the dress over her head, her eyes never leaving mine. We'd make the most of these last moments.

"I want you to put the blackbirds back," she said.

Of all the things I'd painted on her, they were my favorite. I liked that I'd leave her wearing them.

I went to the workstation and opened the door to the paint cupboard, setting what I'd need on a small tray and bringing it over to the cot.

Chill bumps popped out on her legs when I touched her. I rubbed my hands down them, trying to warm her up, my fingers memorizing her. My mouth landed on hers and I forgot about the paint for a second, but I pulled back. As much as I wanted her, I wanted to finish the painting more. Dipping my fingers in the paint, I worked the birds into shape, the slide guitar in the background tracking my movements. I understood why this had been Uncle Hank's favorite song. The birds came quick, like they were flying from my hands. For someone who was good at making mistakes, I could also make something out of nothing.

I knew when I was done that she'd be my masterpiece.

I helped her stand so I could paint the birds on her back. Everywhere my fingers touched, my mouth wasn't far behind. The art was foreplay. Her chest rose and fell with her breaths, and when I was done, my lips were on hers and there was no going back this time. I'd mess up the paint but it didn't matter anymore. It felt right that the paint would smear—it'd be evidence, proof of where I'd been, a stamp of the way I loved her, messy and flawed.

We lay down on the cot and her breathing was loud and

her arms wrapped around me, pulling me closer, always closer. The song had stopped a long time ago but we didn't miss a beat, our bodies still dancing, knowing how to move together.

It was quiet. We were still on the cot. I'd been listening for John, worried he might come in on us, but there was only silence.

June flinched, her whole body tensing up around me. She'd been doing it from time to time all day. I wanted to crawl inside her head and get rid of the intruders. I wanted to tell her that everything would be okay, but I couldn't lie to her. My plan had been to tell her goodbye and slip out after she went to sleep. By morning I'd be long gone and the police would never find me. I figured as long as they got June back, everybody would be happy. Everyone but John.

But I didn't want it to go that way anymore. I knew what I had to do. It was more for me than her. I had to know for sure that she was somewhere safe, where her parents could get to her fast. I couldn't just take off and leave it up to chance. And I needed more time with her.

"We gotta go," I said.

I got up from the cot and started getting dressed.

"Where are we going?"

"I'm taking you up the mountain. We'll take Hank's truck. There won't be roadblocks going that way."

"What? Why?"

"I have to change my plans. John called the police and they'll be here by morning. Where I wanted to go isn't safe anymore. I know of another place, but I have to leave now."

She grabbed my arm. "John called the police? They're coming here?" She looked as panicked as I felt.

"They'll be here by morning, but we aren't waiting for them. I've gotta get out of here now. There's a small police station about an hour up the mountain. I'll drop you there. No one will be expecting us up there. You'll be safe and I'll go farther up the mountain. I'll dump Hank's truck along the way."

I said it with conviction, like it was a plan I'd worked out a long time ago. I worried she'd argue, tell me all the reasons we should stay, tell me that John was right and I should turn myself in, but she stood and said, "Let's go."

We hurried through the workshop but then skidded to a stop. John stood in the doorway. We didn't say anything, just stared at each other. I worried he was going to physically try and stop me from leaving. He was stronger than me. I thought he'd start telling me all the ways I was wrong, all the reasons I needed to listen to him and stay and wait for the police, but he didn't do any of those things.

He stepped to the side, letting us pass. I didn't miss the look on his face, though. It was the same one Hank had worn the last time I saw him.

CHAPTER 19

JUNE

Right after John was deployed, Nick and I were in my bedroom. He'd come to my window, wanting to be let in. We'd been friends for a long time, but this was the first time he'd ever come to my window. Things had been changing between us. He told me things he didn't want anyone else to know. He said that I was good at keeping his secrets and that he trusted me more than anyone. This confession made me feel invincible, like I was taller than mountains.

It was late and he was pacing, making a path from my dresser to the window and back again.

"What's wrong?" I asked.

He shook his head. "Nothing."

But I knew he was lying because he was wearing down the wood planks where he paced. He'd been acting so weird lately, like he was about to tell me something but thought better of it at the last minute. So many times, he'd opened his mouth to say something but then closed it again.

"What?" I asked. "Please tell me what."

I hated that there was something important he needed to say but felt like he couldn't. I worried that he was rethinking his stance that he could trust me with anything.

"You can trust me," I reminded him.

He stopped and stared at me, and the air in the room went still. "I want to be with you," he said. "I want to always be with you."

The ride had been quiet. Part of me couldn't believe that this was really happening, that this was how we'd say goodbye. I was glad I'd worn the yellow dress, because it was right that I should say goodbye to him wearing something he'd given me, covered in blackbirds and paint smears.

We sat in the parking lot of the police station, staring at the sign that read COMMUNITY FIRST. Neither of us said a word or moved an inch. It was rare to know for sure that the next thing you did would change the course of your life forever. We couldn't rush this. We had to make sure we got all the parts just right.

It was a slow day at the police station, because there were only two vehicles in the lot that weren't police cruisers, and one was ours.

Nick hadn't said a word since we'd left his uncle's. He sat facing me, his back to the driver's-side door. In my head, I'd been practicing what came next. I'd get out of the truck and I'd wait in the parking lot until he drove away. I'd wait until I couldn't see his taillights anymore and then I'd wait some more. I had to give him enough time to get away before I walked into the station. Then I'd tell them who I was and they'd call my parents and they'd come get me. Bethany would be with them, because no way could they keep her away, and I'd spend the rest of my life missing Nick.

Nick scooted closer to me. "Remember that day we were at Lake Brady and John was with us and we jumped off the high rock?" he asked.

It was August and the sun had beaten at us from all sides. After we'd gotten the courage to jump off the first time, we'd climbed back up and done it over and over again. We'd gone home sunburned and with muscles already sore.

"Yeah," I said. I moved even closer to him.

"And the time we went to Glow Bowl in Camden and you bowled a thirteen?"

I nodded.

"How does somebody bowl a thirteen?"

"It takes a certain kind of person," I said.

The entire bowling alley had been set up with black lights and we'd found out that one of Bethany's teeth didn't glow in the dark.

"What about the time we saw that band in Eudora? What were they called?"

"Ravaged Melon," I said. "They were terrible."

He agreed. "And all the times we spent in the barn?"

"And every time you painted on me," I said. "I remember everything."

He nodded, like he was just making sure. He reached for my hands. "Promise me something."

"What?"

"Promise me that this won't change things. I need to know that you're still going to college with Bethany, that you're still doing all the things you've planned."

I thought about lying. It would be easier, but I couldn't lie to him on our last day. "I don't even know if I'm going to college."

"Since when?"

"Since I got home from the hospital."

"Don't do that," he said. He looked mad. "Don't give up something you've always wanted just because you can't have it the way you wanted."

"I'm not giving up. But what if I can't do it?"

"What if you can? You're so much stronger than anybody else I know. If I had to pick one person in my life who could do anything, it would be you. You'll figure it out, because that's who you are," he said.

The way he looked at me, I couldn't doubt that he believed what he said. He pulled a folded piece of paper from his bag and unzipped one of the pockets of mine and placed it inside. He didn't explain.

I didn't want to get out of the truck yet. I wanted to tell

him that he was it for me. It would always be him. I thought about our names on the roof of the hospital and what I'd carved in the table at that diner.

Nick touched one of the birds peeking out of the neck of my dress. I'd keep them as long as I could.

"You should go," he said.

"I'm gonna go," I said. I said it like I wasn't leaving him forever.

He nodded and I opened the truck door.

Do you love him? the little girl asked.

Yes.

I stepped down with my bag and turned back to him. I wanted to say something else but I didn't know what my last words to him should be. So I didn't say anything, just shut the door and walked away.

It hurt to breathe. I listened for the sound of the truck's engine cranking up. I waited for it, walking slower. But it didn't come. I heard his door open and I turned around.

What would you do for love? she asked.

He got out of the truck and walked to me, his movements slow. He should be driving away, not walking toward me with his bag.

"What are you doing?" I asked.

"I don't know," he said. "What's right. I think."

"What's that?"

He took my hand and pulled us toward the police station.

"No," I said, planting my feet, stopping us.

No, the little girl begged.

He was supposed to be driving away, not turning himself in.

"You can't do this," I said. "This isn't the right thing. You going to jail isn't right."

He looked down at me and I didn't know how it had happened, but his eyes had aged ten years since he'd gotten out of the truck. "It's where I've always been heading," he said.

He didn't sound sad, just resolved.

"No."

Even if he was right, if what he was doing was right, it felt worse to lose him this way.

"June." He looked away, like he was trying to pick the words that would make me understand. "John is right. He's always right. So was Hank. This is how I make it right, with both of them, and for myself."

He smiled, and tears stung my eyes.

"We both have places to be," he said. "You'll go to college. I'll go to prison. It was what was always going to happen."

He pulled me toward the door and this time I didn't resist. We walked the rest of the way to the entrance of the police station. He opened the door. "Meet up after?"

The front room in the station was small and there was a woman sitting behind a desk. She looked like our school secretary.

"Can I help you?" she asked.

We didn't say anything, just held our breath, waiting for her to recognize us and jump into action.

She didn't, though.

"I'm Nick Hawthorne," Nick said. "And this is June Daniels."

Her eyes flickered with recognition then. She'd heard our names before. A couple of police officers who were behind the desk had, too, because they stopped what they were doing and faced us. All of the air got sucked out of the room.

"Take one step back from the desk," she said.

We stepped back.

"Drop your bags."

We dropped them at our feet.

The police officers moved toward us, their movements measured.

"Don't move," one said.

Nick didn't listen, though. Leaning down, he whispered, "Tell me something new."

He asked me all the time to tell him something he didn't already know about me.

The two cops were still coming toward us, but I had eyes only for Nick. He still waited for my answer.

What does love mean to you? the little girl asked.

She didn't scare me anymore, because I knew what love meant.

"It'll always be you," I said.

He looked so sad, but there was a hint of a smile in the corner of his mouth.

They reached us and grabbed Nick, pulling him away

from me, and I couldn't breathe. My heart tried to beat out of my chest. The little girl was crying now. She loved him, too.

"It's okay, June," Nick said.

But it wasn't.

They pulled him farther away. There was a woman I hadn't noticed before standing next to me, and I felt like I had that night in Leanne Smith's bathroom, like I was dying, like I was going to come out of my skin.

"Come with me," she said.

But I didn't move. I couldn't move. I could only watch them lead him away. My eyes burned.

I noted the tilt of his head and the slope of his neck, how his shoulder blades moved in his back with each step. I watched so closely. I'd be able to draw it later, what he looked like walking away from me.

I thought of all the faces of Nick that I'd known, his little-boy face, his car-thief face, his angry face, his I-love-you face. Now he would have a prison face.

They opened a door and led him into another room. I watched, even after the door closed.

What would you do for love? the little girl asked again. She still cried.

"Anything," I told her.

CHAPTER 20

JUNE

The first time I sat next to Nick at school, we were in the fifth grade. Our teacher, Mrs. Carson, put us together because we were going to be partners on a project. I'd never been that close to him before. He'd drawn on his arm with a pen, intricate designs running from his elbow to his wrist.

I leaned in to get a closer look at them.

"I'm Nick," he said, introducing himself like we hadn't lived in the same small town all our lives.

I liked the formality of it, so I returned the gesture.

"I'm June."

When I got home, I was so sick I couldn't get out of bed. My room was filled with flowers sent from the forty-five churches. They sent cards, too, telling me to get well soon. My parents wanted to put me back in the hospital, but I talked them out of it. Bethany wouldn't leave my side, so she slept on a pallet on my floor. If she got in the bed with me, she'd accidentally move me and I'd get nauseous. My muscles ached and I shook.

Dr. Keels said it looked like withdrawal, but I'd never stopped taking my medication and the drug screen proved I hadn't taken anything else. They didn't know what it was, but I did.

It was Nick. I was sick with missing him.

I'd begged my parents to help Nick. I had worried they'd turn me down because I'd run away with him, but in the end, they'd come through with a good lawyer. He had been able to get Nick's sentence reduced to three years. That meant it would be one thousand ninety-five days before I would touch him again. There were moments when the sentence felt like a victory and moments when it made me so angry, all I saw was red. It wasn't fair that Nick would spend three years of his life in a cell, in a place where I'd watch him grow older through a pane of glass. I wondered how tall he would be when he got out.

Benny Robertson was in county jail, awaiting trial. Nick's lawyer said it looked really bad for him. Other boys who'd worked for him were talking, too, and some men who were already serving time in prison came forward to tell how they'd been recruited from high school, how Benny would pay off some of their parents' debts and make them work it off by stealing for him. Nick's dad was one of them. It wouldn't reduce their sentences, but they said that wasn't why they'd done it. They wanted to make sure that it stopped.

I had an official diagnosis now. I had schizophrenia. As far as my parents knew, I was the first person on either side of my family to have it. I was a pioneer.

Dr. Keels was my psychiatrist. She'd moved from Little Rock to Creed to run the mental health ward at the hospital. It was an offer my dad had made and she couldn't turn it down. He was still moving heaven and earth to try and help me. Our family had a social worker, too. Her name was Martha and she came to check on us from time to time. My mom and dad needed help dealing with everything, too. Martha and my mom were becoming good friends.

Bethany enrolled in Southeastern Arkansas University, and the day she left was one of the hardest days of my life. I was still getting used to dealing when things didn't work out like I'd always imagined, but I wouldn't be left behind forever. My plan was to take two classes next semester. I'd already picked which ones. I was going to ease into the college experience. My parents and I took a couple of trips to the campus so I could get a feel for it. At least twice a week, Bethany FaceTimed me and told me everything that had happened in her classes in minute detail. "So you'll know what to expect when you're ready," she said.

Since my medication had hit peak effect, I hadn't experienced any symptoms, but it wasn't all smooth sailing. I couldn't stop worrying about relapsing. Sometimes the anxiety was harder to manage than the symptoms of psychosis had been, the fear that the sleeping monster would wake again. I started exercising, running, so I'd be so tired at night I couldn't help but sleep. Dr. Keels said as long as I exercised in moderation, it was a good coping strategy.

I hoped she was right.

It was visiting day at the Varner Unit of the Arkansas Department of Correction. It was my first time there. I'd driven myself. I'd gotten my driver's license on my eighteenth birthday. Nick's aunt Linda wasn't able to come this time, but she'd told me what to expect. She'd described what it was like to go through the lines and the metal detectors. She'd told me about the wand they'd use to make sure I wasn't hiding anything. The only thing in my pocket was the piece of paper that Nick had given me right before we turned ourselves in.

The guard looked at the paper, flipped it over, and studied it before handing it back to me.

Nick's aunt had told me they'd lead me into a large room with a glass partition dividing it. She'd said they would tell me where to sit and I would wait. She'd said there'd be a loud buzzing sound and a door would open. She'd said Nick would come through it.

The room was freezing. Any second now, the buzzer would sound and the door would open. I shifted in my seat. It was cold, too. I rested my hand on my pocket, over the piece of paper. I could feel its edges through my jeans. I did that from time to time, reminding myself that it was still there.

On one side of the paper was a map. It showed the way to Hank's cabin from Highway 23 and from there to Nick and John's campsite. The one where he'd wanted to make his home. It looked like the kind of map that might lead to treasure. It even had an *X* marking the spot. I'd studied it. I'd copied it down in my notebook a hundred times. I could draw it with my eyes closed.

On the back was a drawing of a tiny cabin in a clearing surrounded by trees. The cabin was nestled in the side of a mountain, and there was a stream that ran along the edge of the property. The grass was tall and there were sunflowers. It was like the cabin Nick had painted in the barn. All this time, I'd thought it was Hank's cabin, but it wasn't. It was Nick's. The one he'd planned on having, a place that would be permanent.

A girl and a boy were in the drawing. The girl sat on a bench and wrote in her notebook. She had stacks of them at her feet. The boy painted the scene from next to the stream. Blackbirds flew over them, their wings almost touching. It

was beautiful, the kind of place where anything could happen. It was the kind of place that made you believe in happy
endings.

The buzzer sounded.

The door opened.

Any second now.

ACKNOWLEDGMENTS

This is the book I was scared to write. I've always wanted to write a love story, but I didn't expect it to become so personal. There are pieces of my life and my family's life that are so closely woven into the fabric of Nick's and June's characters that it makes me equally excited and terrified to share it with readers.

I understand Nick and his motivations. I understand his family and their poverty, how poverty defines his choices, the fear that you will never overcome it, that even if you do, it will somehow find you again. Thank you to my parents for showing me what it takes to not be defined by your circumstances and endowing me with the grit to overcome them. Thank you for your sacrifices, sleepless nights, and multiple jobs so that my brothers and I could have what you did not.

I battle with depression and anxiety, but unlike June, I do not have schizophrenia. I don't assume that because I have a form of mental illness, I understand what it's like to live with schizophrenia, so I owe a tremendous debt to my sensitivity readers, those with schizophrenia and those in the mental health profession, who provided me with unparalleled insight into the diagnosis and treatment of schizophrenia. It was my goal with June to present her as someone whose diagnosis is a part of her life, but show that her life is not defined by it. It is my hope that with the help of my sensitivity readers, I achieved that. All mistakes are my own.

I must thank Kate McKean, my literary agent. I am so lucky to call her my partner in this writing life. I wouldn't want to do it with anyone else. Thank you to my editor, Melanie Nolan, assistant editor Karen Greenberg, copy editors Artie Bennett and Steph Engel, and cover designers Casey Moses and Regina Flath, who did a fantastic job of putting a face on Nick and June's story. Working with the Knopf team is just as wonderful the second go-round, and I am beyond grateful that I was given the time (I took a lot of it, like years) to make this book the best I could make it. Thanks for allowing me the chance to start over and start over and start over again.

As always, I am indebted to my family and friends; my husband, Erik; and my children, Jake and Eliza, for their unfailing support.

Lastly, thank you to the readers. I hope that you love Nick and June as much as I do.